Second Chance Family

 Horseshoe Home Ranch

LIZ ISAACSON

ISBN-13: 978-1-63876-243-0

"Peace I leave with you, my peace I give unto you: not as the world giveth, give I unto you. Let not your heart be troubled, neither let it be afraid."

— JOHN 14:27

CHAPTER 1

*T*y Barker sang along to the radio as he wound down the canyon, Horseshoe Home Ranch in his rearview mirror. He belted out the lyrics, the tune catchy and the singer's voice in the exact range of Ty's capabilities.

The song ended, and Ty slung his arm out the open window, the whole afternoon ahead of him. "That's a good song, right there, Owen," he said, as if the country music star who used to live in Gold Valley rode shotgun next to him. Of course he didn't, but Ty felt a connection to Owen Carr anyway, mostly because he'd been covering the staff horseback riding lessons at Silver Creek since the cowboy left a couple of summers ago.

Everyone Ty knew had found some way to move on, leave him behind. Caleb had gotten married. Jace and Tom too. There were several cowboys at Horseshoe Home that weren't attached, but they all seemed much younger than

Ty, and he definitely felt isolated from the crowd where he'd once fit.

Another song came on, and Ty exchanged his troubled thoughts for the lyrics he had memorized. The sun shone overhead, and everything in Gold Valley seemed carpeted in shades of green, from the sagebrush surrounding the water-falls, to the lawn framing the church, to the trees towering at the park.

A sense of contentment filled Ty at the familiar sight of the only home he'd ever known. He hadn't left and traveled like some did. He hadn't joined the rodeo. He'd never left Gold Valley; couldn't even understand why someone would want to.

Both of his sisters—one older and one younger—had felt the pull to other parts of the country, leaving Ty here to take care of his parents and the house they'd all grown up in. Ty didn't mind. He liked getting away from the ranch, enjoyed an easy afternoon of mowing the lawn and shaping the shrubbery along his parents' front walk. If he could get the morning chores—which no one wanted on Saturdays except for him—he'd stay in town for the weekend dances that happened all summer long.

Tonight, in fact, and a smile stole across his face. He drove through downtown, his gaze wandering to the park where the dance would be later that evening, the weight of needing more committee members pulling on his mind.

A horn sounded, and Ty refocused his attention forward just in time to see the red light. He slammed on his brakes moments before a blue truck sailed in front of him. His head snapped forward and then back, and his heart catapulted to the base of his throat. "Can't dance if you're dead," he muttered to himself, checking both directions before he inched forward again, even though his light had turned green.

He kept his mind on driving for the rest of the way to Silver Creek, where he arrived with a half hour to spare before the riding lessons began. After walking around the barn from the parking lot, he entered it and moved down the row of horses, greeting them all as if they were old friends.

Ty paused outside Pompeii's stall—which was empty. The patients at Silver Creek didn't ride on Saturdays, so the horse shouldn't have been gone. Ty glanced around, his pulse skipping ahead of itself once more.

"Where is he?" he asked a smaller horse named Kimchi. "He's all right, isn't he?" Ty considered horses as much his friends as humans, and his concern for the tall quarter horse spiked.

He vaulted the fence and landed in Pompeii's stall, moving quickly toward the back opening that led to an outdoor arena. Though his boots made clomping noises against the cement, he could distinctly hear the uneven rhythm of horse's hooves as he approached the arena.

Sure enough, a woman rode Pompeii in the arena, her hair fanning out like a fantastic white-blonde curtain behind her. He couldn't see her face, but he could see she didn't quite know how to get Pompeii to do what she wanted. The horse's gait was stilted, and she yanked on the reins when she wanted him to go right, but he didn't.

Ty climbed the rungs on the fence and sat on the top one. "You're squeezin' 'im too tight," he called.

The woman swung toward him, surprise etched across her face. She yelped as Pompeii also turned his attention to Ty—and then headed right for him.

Shock traveled through Ty as the horse rose into a gallop, and he scrambled over the fence just as Pompeii arrived, skidding to a stop and throwing the woman from his back.

Her scream embedded itself into Ty's ears, his mind, his very soul, before she landed right on top of him.

They both collapsed to the ground in a flurry of limbs and grunts. Ty ended up on the bottom, the woman's elbow digging painfully into his ribs, and her knee where no one's knee should ever be.

Ty tried to hold still as pain radiated through his body from sole to skull, but the woman scrambled around, her limbs made of sharp points and sudden movements. He groaned as her elbow made contact with his stomach.

"What was that?" she sputtered, trying desperately to find somewhere to lean her weight that wasn't part of Ty. He'd appreciate that too, to tell the truth. In the end, she pressed both palms against his chest and pushed herself up.

The air rushed from Ty's lungs, and he emitted a strangled sound as she gained her feet and started brushing off her decidedly city clothes. How she could move and breathe in jeans so tight and a blouse so silky almost seemed beyond Ty's reasoning.

He took a few extra seconds to find a decent lungful of air, to realize that the aches in his muscles were just that—aches. Not breaks.

"You were squeezin' 'im too tight," Ty drawled again as he got himself into a seated position. The woman's bright blue eyes seemed so familiar, but he hadn't seen hair so silvery-white on someone her age ever. "I was just trying to help."

"Yeah, help me get thrown."

Pompeii pawed the ground and Ty said, "I wouldn't go back in there quite yet," as the woman started to duck to go under the rungs. He got to his feet and dusted himself down. "He's not interested in riding right now."

"Thanks to you."

Ire rose in Ty. "Who are you? Why are you out here ridin' one of the horses by yourself?"

The woman shook out her hair and squared her shoulders. "I'm new here. I was waiting for the riding instructor, and thought I'd give it a try."

Ty's eyebrows shot up. "You thought you'd give riding a horse *a try?*"

"I rode when I was younger." She rolled her right shoulder—Ty wondered if it ached the way his did—and trained those aquamarine eyes of hers right on his. Ty forgot his own name for a moment. Because he'd suddenly remembered hers.

"River Lee?"

She flinched, and dark shutters drew themselves over those crystal clear eyes. "I go by River now."

Every organ in Ty's body danced the tango. River Lee Whitely had returned to Gold Valley. His heart remembered the last time he'd seen her, and it clenched painfully at the same time hope soared through him.

"River Lee Whitely." He chuckled and shook his head, his usual playfulness rising within him. "You didn't *ride* when you were younger."

"I've been on a horse before, Ty."

So she remembered him too. He wondered if her memories were as strong as his, as saturated with the color and sound of the fair, the taste of that caramel apple they'd shared—and the kiss that followed it.

Ty swallowed hard, his fantasies suddenly overwhelming his memories. "But you didn't ride," he said. "If I remember right, you sat right behind me in the saddle, no work necessary." He slid her a playful smile, wondering—and hoping—it would work as well now as it had fifteen years ago.

Judging by the insta-scowl on her face, his smile had lost some of its charm. A ripple of unease tripped through Ty. "Well," he said. "I'm your riding instructor today, but the lesson doesn't start for another twenty minutes."

———

River blinked at Ty, sure she'd heard him wrong. *He* was her riding instructor? Half of her wanted to march over to the office and demand someone else. She knew it would be pointless. The director of Silver Creek, Dr. Richards, didn't work weekends. The office wasn't even open as only a skeleton staff stayed on-site through the weekends. And she had to be trained with horses to keep the job.

Another set of blue eyes danced through her mind. Her daughter, Lexi's. And another pair: Hannah's. River needed this job, for herself and her two daughters.

She blinked and breathed, and when she looked at Ty again, his stunning, sunny hazel eyes stared back at her, no blue in sight. She could take riding lessons from him. It wasn't like they'd be dating or anything.

"I'll get Pompeii back in his stall." Ty went over the fence, not through it like River was going to, and held the horse's reins in his hand before River had even moved. The horse didn't snort or paw at him, and he spoke to it like it was his grandmother, soothing and low and with a slight coo in his voice.

River shouldn't have been surprised. Ty Barker had always had a way with horses, with dogs—and with girls. River remembered their fun-filled summer together, those hot nights they walked around the town and up to the waterfalls, the single kiss she'd shared with him.

"You comin'?"

She shook herself out of the memory and found him already at the door leading inside. She strode after him despite the hitch of pain in her right ankle and the slight discomfort in her shoulders, wishing she looked more like a resident of Gold Valley instead of where she'd come from: Las Vegas.

At least it was summer in Montana, and she didn't need to buy a whole new wardrobe for a few more months. "Why do we have to take him back?" she asked.

"Well, for starters, you didn't put his saddle on right. So that needs to be redone. And secondly, you're not the only person in the lesson. It's a group lesson, and I was told there were four of you starting today."

"Four of us?" River had only been back in town for a week, and she'd only signed her employment paperwork on Wednesday. She'd start with a group of girls on Monday, and Dr. Richards wanted her to learn to ride a horse over the next twelve weeks—just like the girls did when they came to Silver Creek.

"This place turns over counselors like they're pancakes." Ty led the horse back into his stall while River took the path between two stalls and out to the front of the barn.

"They do?" River hated that everything she'd said had been a question.

"It's a tough job," he said.

Fear boiled inside her, along with a healthy helping of indignation. "Have you done it?"

He laughed, the sound as full and glorious as it had been when River was a teenager. She shivered and a spring of desire to hear his chuckle again bubbled up inside her. She couldn't believe a noise she hadn't heard in a long, long time could elicit such a strong reaction from her. Like the lyrics of a song, his laugh had never left her mind, even if she couldn't recall it at will.

"I work at Horseshoe Home," he said. "I only do this on

the weekends." He scanned her, a hint of something mischievous in his eye. She shifted her feet, noticing how his muscles filled out his shoulders, his arms, his chest. He'd been broad as a sixteen-year-old, but skinny. Now he had the form of a man who worked a ranch and tamed wild horses in his spare time. And she had a new hair color, two daughters under the age of five, and her old bedroom in her parents' house.

"So, what brings you back to town?" he asked as he removed the offensive saddle and redid the work.

River opened her mouth to answer, glad when two other men showed up before she could speak. They both wore cowboy hats and boots, and once again, River felt completely misdressed.

"You must be Ty," one of them said. He shook hands with Ty over the railing and then glanced at River. "I'm Rueben."

Introductions were made, and conversations started, and River did her best to paint her smile in place and speak only when spoken to. Her strategy worked, and before she knew it, Ty had paired her with a much smaller, red-haired horse named, believe it or not, Ole Red.

CHAPTER 2

*R*iver's whole body ached by the time she dismounted—clumsily, too. She'd tripped on the stirrup and practically fallen on top of Ty for a second time that day. Her ankle throbbed now, but she'd made it to her car without limping. She would not give Ty the opportunity to tease her, or worse, offer his help.

She didn't need anyone's help, thank you very much. John, her ex-husband, had agreed to have the child support for Lexi and Hannah automatically withdrawn from his hefty paychecks from the law firm in Vegas where he still worked. Still with the same secretary too.

Bitterness coated River's tongue, but it didn't last long. Her marriage had ended eighteen months ago, and the divorce itself was a year old. She'd stayed in Las Vegas out of a legal obligation not to leave the state until everything regarding the girls was settled.

And that had happened a month ago. River had

promptly packed everything they owned and returned to Gold Valley. Her mom had been begging her to come home since the day she'd left for college. A single mother herself, River's mother had been by River's side since the beginning of the split. River wasn't ashamed to admit that she'd been relying on her mom for more than just a place to stay for a while now.

When she pushed into the house with a couple of bags of groceries, she found her two tow-headed girls sitting at the table, a plastic cup of discolored water sitting between them as they painted with watercolors. "Hey, sweeties," she said, removing the tired notes from her voice. She bent over and gave each daughter a quick kiss on the cheek before setting the groceries on the counter. "Where's Grandma?"

Her mother had retired last year, which made the horse-back riding lessons do-able. Or so River had thought.

"She's in the backyard," Lexi said. "Someone came to visit."

River cocked an eyebrow at the sliding glass door that led to the backyard that was her mother's pride and joy. She kept large beds of flowers with lilies, poppies, and roses in a variety of colors. In the far left corner, she'd planted several lilac bushes and two bleeding heart trees that River had grown up loving. She often hid behind the lilacs in the summer when she wanted to be alone, breathing in their fragrance and trying to figure out what to do with her life.

With the strong urge to lose herself in that scent again, River stepped to the door and slid it open. "Stay here, girls. I'll be right back to make dinner." She'd just come in from the heated afternoon, but the sweat on her brow had barely cooled in the weak air conditioning.

"Mom?" She glanced around but didn't see her mother. The grass stretched before her like an emerald carpet, and Pippa, her mother's white terrier yipped and came trotting around the shed that sat under the towering bur oak tree. Her little legs pumped as she crossed the lawn.

"Hey, Pip." River scooped up the little, fifteen-pound dog and added, "Where's Mommy, huh?"

As the seconds stretched, River's anxiety expanded. Surely her mother wouldn't just wander off and leave her two granddaughters in the house alone. Just as she was about to return to the house and call her mother—and then the Sheriff—the door to the shed flew open and banged against the building.

Her mother exited, a wide smile on her face. Her trilling laugh echoed through the quiet neighborhood, easing River's worry—until she saw the tall, broad cowboy who ducked to exit the shed behind her mother.

Then she could only see red. She stomped toward the shed, where Ty stood with a shovel slung over his shoulder, that knee-weakening smile adorning his beautiful mouth.

"What are you doing here?" she demanded.

He switched his happy gaze to hers, and she remembered how jovial he'd always been. Some might even call him a prankster, though he never did anything harmful. At least that he'd been caught for.

"Hey, River Lee," he said easily, like he hadn't given her the best kiss of her life and then broken up with her.

"It's just River," she ground between her teeth. "And you didn't answer my question."

"I wanted to ask you something, but you weren't here." He glanced at River's mom. "And your mom asked me to do some yard work for her."

River switched her glare to her mother, the traitor. "You don't need any yard work done."

Her mother lifted her chin, her blue eyes as dangerous as Ty's dark ones. Glittering just as much too. "Yes, I do. I haven't been able to get that faucet to stop leaking. Ty said he could do it."

River stared past the two of them to the spigot in the back of the yard, surrounded by white, decorative rocks. Her gaze landed back on Ty, who had taken the smile from knee-weakening to bone-melting. "With a shovel?" she asked, a definite bite of acid in her question.

He tipped his hat, said, "You never know when you'll need a shovel," and strode toward the leaking faucet.

"Mom," River hissed as Pippa began squirming in her arms. She set the little dog down and she tore after Ty. "How long has he been here?"

She didn't take her eyes from Ty's back. "I don't know. Fifteen minutes? The girls are inside."

"I saw them." River spun and retraced her steps back to the house. Did her mother honestly think River wanted to start dating again?

Maybe if the man asking is Ty Barker.

She almost tripped over her own feet at the way her brain betrayed her. She gave herself a shake and practically ripped the sliding glass door off its track. Once inside the house, her chest heaved as if she'd just run a marathon. She wasn't even sure why. The faucet *had* been leaking since the irrigation water had come back on, but it wasn't like her mother had even tried to fix it herself. She just hadn't gotten around to it, what with River and her daughters moving in with such little notice.

She yanked the groceries out of the bags and picked up a chef's knife to chop the onions she needed for the sloppy Joes. Hannah giggled, and River's anger deflated.

"Pippa," the little girl said, sliding off her chair and straining to open the sliding glass door. River let her have the chance to let the dog in, smiling with pride when Hannah got the door open and beamed in River's direction.

"Good job, baby," River said, her dialect already returning to the small-town, western way of talking she'd left behind long ago.

"I cook too?" Hannah toddled into the kitchen, and River pulled over the chair she'd been sitting on. After lifting Hannah onto it and setting a heavy pan on the stove, she gave her a wooden spoon.

"You stir." She mimicked moving the spoon around the pan and turned back to the counter to collect the chopped onions. They sizzled as they hit the pan, and Hannah started stirring the way River had shown her.

River added salt and pepper, as well as a hunk of butter, and stepped around Hannah to open the fridge. She'd collected the ground beef, the mustard, and the chili sauce before she heard voices approaching.

A low, masculine one that sent shivers down her spine and her mother's higher timbre that grated against River's nerves. Truth be told, she was just as annoyed at herself for finding every single thing about Ty so darn attractive.

She eyed him as he entered the house and took in the scene before him: Lexi painting at the table, the same eyes and nose as River. And Hannah standing at the stove, her hair the exact same color as River's, even if River's came from multiple steps only a talented stylist could achieve.

"Beef," River said quietly as she turned her back on Ty and started crumbling the beef into the pan so Hannah could stir it around. "Mix it all up, 'kay?" She steadfastly refused to look at Ty as she got out a bottle of apple cider vinegar and a sack of brown sugar.

He had come by to ask her something, but she didn't want to talk to him. Over the past couple of years, River had gotten very good at ignoring uncomfortable things and making light of awkward situations.

She'd also learned how to talk about how she felt, and she'd already looked for a therapist here in Gold Valley that could continue to help her heal emotionally.

"Can I talk to you for a sec?" Ty seemed to appear magically at his side, as if he'd teleported there.

River's fingers stumbled on the twist tie keeping the brown sugar fresh. Instead of trying to rectify her mistake, she simply abandoned the task. "Mom? Can you stand here by Hannah?" The beef needed to brown, and that was at least five or six minutes away.

"Sure thing." Her mom edged into the kitchen as Ty slid

his way out. He walked into the living room, but didn't stop there. He opened the front door stepped onto the porch.

River warred with herself. She could rush to the door and lock it, sending a clear and loud message to Ty—the way he had all those summers ago.

Don't burn bridges, echoed in her mind. One of her mother's life lessons. One that had actually stuck in River's mind. One she'd relied on throughout college, her counseling internship, even her failed marriage.

She coached herself that just because Ty was good-looking didn't mean she had to let him into her life. That just because she'd kissed him before didn't mean she had to do it again. That just because he wanted to talk didn't mean she had to listen.

She lifted her shoulders and joined him on the front porch. "What's up?"

Ty leaned against the porch railing, seemingly at ease right here where he hadn't been for a while. "So just hear me out."

It took every ounce of River's willpower not to lean her elbows next to his, share the same air as him, take a deep drag of his intoxicating scent. "All right."

"All right," he drawled, mimicking her. "You sound like you haven't left at all." He chuckled but sobered quickly. "So I help out with the summer activities. Specifically, I'm in charge of the children's carnival during the Fourth of July week, the end-of-summer carnival, and the weekend dances."

River tried to bite down on the information and chew

on it for a moment before speaking, but trying to imagine Ty planning events was so far from who she thought he was. "You're doing what?" she asked with no small measure of incredulity.

His shoulders stiffened and he ducked his chin to put the brim of his cowboy hat between them. "I volunteer on a community service committee," he said. "And we need more help. I thought maybe you'd like to join up. Help out with the kid's activities or the carnival or the dances."

She laughed, the sound anything but carefree and happy. "I don't think so." She'd be working with a group of eight teen girls come Monday, and then returning home to care for her own two daughters. She didn't think she'd even have enough mental stamina to do that, let alone think about what other people's children would like to see and do at an Independence Day activity.

And helping with the carnival? Definitely out. Just thinking about such things made the taste of caramel coat her tongue and her lips tingle from the once-gentle pressure of Ty's mouth against hers.

No, she could absolutely not help him organize anything having to do with the carnival. No, sirree.

She'd known about the dances in Gold Valley's central square. She'd attended as a teenager, spun with several boys before she left for college, even snuck off to kiss one of them after the last dance of the summer.

River glanced at Ty, wondering if those memories, that summer, his words, ever haunted him.

"You don't have to do all of that," Ty said. "Just one thing would suffice. Or I know Doris Downing needs help with the judging for the county fair. Baked goods and sewing."

The way he wouldn't look at her drove frustration through her bloodstream. At the same time, she didn't want his powerful gaze on her, sure she'd wilt beneath the magnificence of his murky, pond water-colored eyes.

He waited with all the patience of a monk, and River couldn't stand to be in the same space as him for much longer. "Thanks, but no thanks." She twisted, entered the house, and closed the door behind her.

Exhaling, she leaned into the door and pressed her eyes closed. *Dear Lord,* she prayed. *How am I going to survive living in Gold Valley with Ty Barker?*

God didn't have an answer for her, and River felt as though she'd been stung by an army of red ants. She thought she'd be able to find a new start in Gold Valley. Thought she'd be able to find peace away from the hustle and bustle of the big cities where she used to live. Thought she'd be able to build a life for her girls and raise them with good values.

She had not even considered that Ty would still be in town, though she should have known better. A country boy at heart, she couldn't imagine Ty anywhere with more people than cattle. A city like Las Vegas would swallow him whole. It had River, and she loved a thriving city, with more than one grocery store and highways and byways that criss-crossed the metropolis.

"Mama," Hannah said, and River opened her eyes, choosing to put one foot in front of the other, just like she had when she'd left Las Vegas. Along with that, she believed if she kept her faith in the Lord, He'd guide her where she needed to go.

She scraped her hair off her forehead and gave Hannah a tired smile. "Look at what you've done, baby doll." She stroked the little girl's hair and said, "Now we add everything and then you'll keep stirring."

———

Ty's disappointment over River's laughter and subsequent rejection wafted behind him like a foul scent. His mother noticed when he arrived at their house, and she questioned him relentlessly until he muttered something about the lawn and escaped to the backyard.

Honestly, he wasn't sure why he'd thought asking River to get involved with community service was a good idea. He just knew he'd felt like he should, so he'd jumped in his truck and gone to her mother's house. Seeing the two blonde girls hanging onto their grandmother's legs had taken the wind right out of his sails. And yet, he'd still asked River if she'd wanted to help, as if she didn't already have her hands full.

The roar of the lawnmower kept Ty's mutterings mute to the rest of the world. As he berated himself for such grand notions, he clipped his parents' yard to pure perfection. He showered, and denied his mother the opportunity to feed him dinner—a rare occurrence indeed. If she hadn't known something was off then, she certainly would've when he bypassed the homemade waffles and plate of bacon.

"What's wrong?" She put her hands on her hips and cocked her head at him, her dark eyes blazing with determination.

"Nothin', Ma. Don't want to talk about it." He picked up a waffle and smeared peanut butter on it like it was a piece of bread. "I will eat here."

"Everything okay at the ranch?"

"Nothing ever changes at the ranch." He took a big bite of his waffle sandwich, thinking he should just tell him mom about River Lee. She'd find out anyway, and if he just blurted it out, he wouldn't have to endure the questioning.

"The riding lessons, then?" She spoke with a quietness in her tone but with eyes so sharp they cut right through Ty's defenses.

He shook his head, swallowed, and said, "Did you know River Lee Whitely is back in town? And that she has two daughters?"

Everything about his mom softened. She glanced over Ty's shoulder as his dad entered the kitchen. "I had heard she was back, yes."

"Who's back?" His dad slid a waffle onto a plate and slathered it with butter.

"River Lee Whitely," his mom said before Ty could somehow communicate with her nonverbally.

"River Lee?" His dad abandoned his waffle prep and pinned Ty with a look. "You're still hung up on her?"

Ty grabbed a handful of bacon and put it on a plate. "I was never 'hung up' on her, Dad."

"You were sneakin' out all the time to see her."

"Once," Ty said. "I snuck out once. And it wasn't like I was twelve years old."

"Doesn't matter how old you were." He spooned sugared strawberries onto his waffle. "Bein' older is worse. No control over your hormones."

Ty scoffed and took his food to the table. His mom watched the exchange with too much interest, and Ty had the urge to get out of the house as quickly as possible. He shoved the rest of his waffle in his mouth and chewed with vigor. The waffle scraped his throat as he practically swallowed it whole.

"I have to go."

"Have fun," his mom said, while his dad added, "Be good."

Ty waved to indicate that he'd heard them, but every step he took was fueled by frustration. So he'd snuck out once to meet River Lee at the drive-in. He didn't have a car, but she did. Nothing had happened. In fact, he'd barely slipped his fingers between hers before his dad had pounded on the window and demanded Ty get out of the sedan.

Even after that embarrassing incident, River Lee had still been interested in him. If only she hadn't said she couldn't wait to leave Gold Valley. Couldn't wait to start college. Couldn't wait to "get on with her life."

She'd told him all of that after he'd taken her on the

Ferris wheel, after he'd bought a caramel apple to share, after they'd danced around the square, after they'd snuck off to a secret spot behind the rodeo stands and kissed. They'd found a patch of grass illuminated by the moonlight and lay in each other's arms, whispering secrets until long past his curfew.

And she'd done exactly what she'd said she wanted to do. She'd left Gold Valley. She'd gone to college. She'd gotten on with her life.

A life that didn't include him.

Even after he'd kissed her, she hadn't made room for him in her life. He'd held her anyway, smiled at her dreams anyway, told her he'd see her later anyway.

And he had seen her. But he hadn't touched her again. Hadn't kissed her more than that one, magical time behind the rodeo stands, her words always a barrier between them. Then...but maybe not now.

A smile graced Ty's face, and he wondered if maybe God had led River Lee home right when she was supposed to be here.

He arrived at the park and helped set up the refreshment tables, the dance floor, and the sound equipment for the band. It was a big job for only a handful of people, and he was certain everything would be easier with only one more pair of hands.

River Lee's hands.

Forget about it, Ty, he told himself just before a brunette launched herself at him with a squeal and the strength of a python in her legs as she wrapped them around his body.

"There you are," she said with more flirt in her voice than anything else. "I've missed you."

Ty held onto Whitney, because he had little other choice. Number one, he didn't want to drop the girl. Number two, technically, one could say they were dating. Ty had asked her to dance two weeks ago, and then taken her for ice cream afterward. And at last week's shindig, he hadn't danced with anyone but her and they'd gone stargazing at the waterfalls after the festivities ended.

But with the reappearance of River Lee in his life, he'd completely, one-hundred percent forgotten about Whitney. He groaned and pretended it was because of her body attached to his. But really, it was the sound of his heart dying just a little bit.

CHAPTER 3

*T*y rose with the sun, his muscles anxious for a few hours of good hard work. He adored the morning chores, the way the world awakened to golden light, the stillness and silence of the sunbeams on snow or sod.

He'd slept poorly the night before, after a long dance filled with glances to make sure River Lee didn't show up and see him dancing with someone else. He'd lain in bed, wondering why he cared. She'd made it pretty clear how she felt about reuniting with him, and it wasn't like he could keep his reputation a secret. He'd been out with almost every eligible woman in Gold Valley under age forty. In fact, he'd all but given up on finding someone he wanted to spend longer than a few hours with.

Because of his work on the ranch, he didn't see his girl-friends all that much, which was usually just fine by him. But as he filled the bull watering troughs, and took horses

27

out to pastures, and rode a four-wheeler out to check on the nearest segment of the herd, all he could think about was the next time he could see River Lee.

He returned to his cabin in time to shower and leap down his front steps just as Caleb and Holly climbed into her truck. "Can I catch a ride with y'all?"

Caleb scanned him from the tips of his boots to the tie he wore loosely around his neck. He started to work it into the proper knot while Caleb appraised him. "Sure thing."

Holly already rode immediately next to Caleb, so Ty climbed into the cab and pulled the door closed behind him. "Thanks."

It wasn't an anomaly for Ty to go to church. Sometimes he did, and sometimes he didn't. So why was Caleb giving him that look with the glint in his eye?

"What?" he finally asked.

"Nothing," Caleb said, focusing his attention out the windshield again.

But his best friend's *nothing* was definitely *something*. Ty didn't want to get into whatever it was at the moment, so he simply looked out his window and enjoyed the easiness of being with his friends on the way to church.

People streamed from the parking lot into the building with the stained glass window that Ty had always loved. A few years ago, another cowboy on the ranch, Landon Edmunds, had organized the community to clean the window. Ty had been the first in line, and it was from that service that he'd started volunteering in the community. He'd started small, with judging the cattle at the county fair. Last year, he'd done that as well as helped to organize and set up the carnival. And this year, he was in charge of several summer activities. His community service felt all-encompassing and overwhelming, but Ty still enjoyed it.

"Earth to Ty." Caleb chuckled as Ty swung his gaze toward him and found he and Holly had already gotten out of the truck and were looking at him expectantly. "Wow, whoever she is, she must be somethin' special." Caleb closed the door, another chuckle already in the space between them.

Ty scrambled from the truck and caught up to his friend. "There's no girl."

"Right," Caleb scoffed. "The only time I've ever seen you with such a dreamy look was after you kissed Harli Baugh after the fireworks a coupla years ago. And she wasn't even your date."

Ty's stomach turned over, and not in a good way. "It's not a girl," he repeated. River Lee wasn't just any girl. Not a girl he'd meet at a Saturday night dance in the summer heat. Not a girl he'd kiss just because he could.

She was a woman. A year older than him, with two little girls to take care of. A degree in professional counseling, with a near-perfect score on her psychology exam, if her mother was to be believed. Ty knew River Lee was smart, and he didn't doubt her mother's claims. She'd told him all about River Lee while he fixed her faucet. Apparently, she'd taken the job at Silver Creek—the first job where she'd actually use the master's degree she'd earned from UNLV. She was only waiting for approval from the state of Montana to practice legally.

No, River Lee was not just a girl. At least Ty had spoken true on that point.

He entered the church, more grateful for air conditioning than anything else at that moment, and scanned the lobby for that shock of white-blonde hair. He didn't find it, and his heart sank as if someone had tied a weight to it.

A familiar giggle caught his attention and he turned toward Whitney. She tossed her dark hair over her shoulder and sauntered toward him in a dress two sizes too small. "Hey, cowboy."

He let her trip her fingers up his chest, but he didn't smile at her the way he normally would have. "Whitney, we need to talk."

"Oh." Her demeanor fell, and Ty felt like the jerkiest jerk on the planet. Was he really going to break up with her at church? Did he need to break up with her at all? He hadn't kissed her. He'd danced with her a few times and taken a walk along the boardwalk at the waterfalls. Did that mean they were dating?

"I'm just not sure this is working," he said. "I like you, don't get me wrong, I just...." River Lee entered the building, each of her hands claimed by one of her daughters. She wore a long, flowing black dress that bore the bright blue and green feathers of a peacock. The fabric made her hair seem whiter and brighter than before, and the look suited her well. Ty froze, his words lodged somewhere between his brain and his voice box.

River Lee didn't glance around. Didn't wait to see if anyone was watching her. He wondered if she'd been in town long enough to come to church prior to this, as he hadn't attended in a couple of weeks.

She moved without hesitation toward the chapel doors and disappeared, the little girls going with her. Ty's heart felt like a machine gun in his chest, firing against his ribs with too much force and too much speed.

Ty's feet wanted to follow her, and follow fast. He took a single step before he realized Whitney was still attached to his arm. Thankfully, he didn't think River Lee had seen him.

"Can we talk later?" he asked as Jace and Belle entered the chapel with their son, Tucker. "I need to talk to my boss." He prayed for forgiveness for the little white lie as he hurried across the foyer and attached himself to Jace. "Hey," he whispered, just so he wouldn't be a total liar.

"Mornin' Ty." Jace paused and took a longer look at him. "What's eatin' you?"

Ty shook his head, his annoyance near its peak already and the service hadn't even started yet. To make matters worse, River Lee had slid onto a crowded bench beside to her mother, her girls taking up all the space next to her.

But his luck took a turn when he spied Caleb on the row directly in front of River Lee—and he'd saved the end spot for Ty. He clapped Jace on the shoulder and strode toward the bench, his heart doing that strange gunshot thing again.

He sank into the spot and sighed, "Thanks, Caleb," just loud enough for River Lee to hear. He watched her out of the corner of his eye, and he witnessed the moment she saw him. Her right hand fluttered up to her throat before she busied herself with her oldest daughter.

"Oh, hey, River Lee," he said, pretending to notice her for the first time. "You look real nice." He turned his attention to the girls. "Hey, Lexi." The little girl looked up and gave him a shy smile. "Remember me?"

She glanced at River Lee, who wore a look somewhere between annoyance and acceptance. Ty would take it. "Go on, missy. Remember your manners."

"Hello, Mister Ty." Lexi dropped her gaze immediately afterward, and a chuckle broke free from Ty's throat.

Ty wanted to soak in River Lee's beauty, and ask her mother to slide over a seat so he could squeeze onto the bench, and hold her hand in secret. But he knew when to hold his cards and when to play them, so he flashed her another smile and turned around.

The pastor got up to welcome everyone at the same time Caleb leaned over and said, "Not a girl, huh?"

"Trust me," Ty whispered. "River Lee Whitely is *not* a girl."

"Oh, I can see that." Caleb cast a glance behind them, and Ty wanted to pinch him until he faced the front. "And did you say River Lee?"

"Shout it, why don't you?" Ty hissed. "Yes, River Lee."

"*The* River Lee you told me about?"

"When did I tell you about her?"

"When you said you'd already kissed the girl of your dreams, and you were worried you'd never get to do it again."

Ty straightened his tie, a flash of fear and unease flowing through him. He shrugged it off, not remembering ever telling Caleb about the life-changing kiss with River Lee.

"I didn't tell you that."

Caleb's chuckle got lost under the deep bass voice of the pastor, but even the sermon couldn't erase Ty's relentless thoughts of kissing River Lee again.

River's back ached with how straight she sat, and she forced a measure of relaxation through her shoulders and down into her core muscles. Wasps still swarmed in her stomach, no matter how many times she tried to focus on the pastor, no matter that she kept her gaze straight forward during the rest hymn, no matter that Ty didn't lean over and whisper with his cowboy friend, Caleb Chamberlain, again.

Yes, River knew them both, and she hadn't experienced even an ounce of surprise to find them sitting by one another, their cowboy hats perched in place. The brunette bombshell on Caleb's arm—and sporting his diamond ring —had garnered a bit of surprise for River. Not that Caleb wasn't a great guy. He just seemed...more carefree than marriage usually required.

Like Ty.

She ground her teeth together at the constant way he inserted himself into her mind. Though she'd really liked Ty in high school, she had never really considered him to be someone she could get serious with. And if the rumors she'd heard around town could be believed, he'd dated everyone with a double X-chromosome, further cementing her opinion of him as someone who played around but wasn't looking to settle down.

She'd heard about his current girlfriend from the cashier at McCall's, the gas station that housed more gossip than chocolate. She'd heard about three of his ex-girlfriends when she went to see her friend, Katie, at the salon. Of course, both places in Gold Valley were well-known for their rumors, most of which weren't true. But with the multiple sources—and from the mouth of one woman who dated Ty for exactly ten days before he told her he just "didn't feel good" about her—River had believed the rumors.

She hadn't known what not feeling good about someone meant, and River had been thinking about it since her hair appointment the week before. Of course, she hadn't expected to really run into Ty much, what with him living and working thirty minutes up the canyon, at Horseshoe Home Ranch.

Her tailbone screamed a shout of pain, a reminder of the horseback riding lessons she'd have to endure for the next eleven weeks. She shifted on the hard bench, letting her daughters distract her from the sermon.

But they couldn't distract her from Ty long enough for her to draw a decent breath, one that wasn't filled with the unfairly delicious scent of his cologne. Men really shouldn't be allowed to use products filled with metallic and musky scents. And all that sandalwood? All that cedar?

River shook her head, completely defenseless against Ty's scent. She wanted to dive into him, roll around, get coated in all that honeyed, spicy smell, and then never bathe again. As consumed with him as she was, she didn't even realize when the sermon ended and the congregation stood. She hurried to get Lexi's coloring book cleaned up and Hannah's sippy cup back in the diaper bag.

By the time she finished, nearly everyone had vacated the chapel. A low din echoed back to her from the lobby, where churchgoers loitered to chat with one another before heading out into the summer heat.

She finally herded Hannah and Lexi into the aisle, her mother waiting patiently behind her. They moved slowly toward the crowd, and River wished she'd been ready to go sooner so she could've beaten everyone out the doors.

Didn't matter. She had agreed to go to the monthly picnic that afternoon. She was even making cheddar biscuits for the occasion, and her mother had baked her Gold Valley-famous chocolate cake that morning. Once that beauty was frosted, she'd be ready to sink into sugar-coated bliss, no room for Ty and his perfectly tailored slacks, that bright blue tie, and that dangerous-to-her-health cowboy hat.

She'd taken one step out of the building when Ty emerged from the very bricks themselves. "So I heard you were going to the picnic," he said, settling into stride next to her. "Is that true?"

"Who did you hear that from?" She barely gave him a glance, choosing instead to lean away so she wouldn't catch a whiff of that cologne that clouded her reasoning skills.

"Katie. She's Caleb's sister, and she said—"

River stopped and stared, all thoughts of protecting herself from his good looks, his tantalizing scent, gone. "Katie?" That little traitor! She'd said nothing while she bleached and colored River's hair last week. Nothing about her brother. Nothing about Ty. They didn't talk about men —all the women around them had. Plus, River wasn't especially interested in detailing why her marriage had ended. For the sake of her daughters, she tried to be nothing but positive about John, though he'd betrayed her in the worst way possible—repeatedly.

"Right, Katie." Ty reached back and tapped two fingers to the back of his cowboy hat, tipping it further forward on his forehead. "So I thought maybe I could eat with you."

"I—"

"I usually go alone, and I don't like just sort of sitting on the end next to some family. But I thought...."

She really wanted him to finish that sentence, find out what he thought. She remained silent, refusing to give him a way out of his own mouth.

"You thought what?" she prompted.

"I thought maybe we could go together." He shoved his hands in his pockets and rocked back and forth from heel to toe. Heel to toe. Heel to toe. "Look, I gotta go. I caught a ride with Caleb and Holly." He glanced over his shoulder as a pickup truck pulled up to the curb. "I'll give you my number, and you can let me know if I can eat with you. I have to go anyway, but it would be nice not to have to search for somewhere to belong." He pulled out his phone and said, "What's your number?"

"Excuse me?"

"So I can send you my number," he said, a hint of innocence in his voice but that devilish glint right there in those dark hazel eyes.

She sighed, tired of resisting him when everything in her wanted to just give in. She recited her number, and Ty grinned, tapped on his phone, and said, "Great." He took off as if he'd been launched from a slingshot, practically leaping into the truck from ten feet away. His laughter floated back to her and made the hair on her arms stand up. Goosebumps broke out on her skin in anticipation of sitting next to him at the picnic.

"So." Her mother linked her arm through River's and got her feet moving. "Are you going to sit by him at the picnic?"

River shook her head, her first reaction to say no. But she'd be there anyway. Was she really going to deny him from having somewhere to sit?

"Does he help with the picnics too?" she asked.

"This is the first one of the summer," her mom said. "So maybe."

"He didn't say that when he asked me to help."

Her mom shrugged, and they all loaded into her car. River wished she was driving so she couldn't fiddle with her phone. Couldn't flip it over, and over, and over, almost expecting Ty to text her, maybe with another plea to sit with her.

She finally just let her thumbs do what they wanted, with little direction from her heart. After all, that organ had led her astray before. Maybe she shouldn't be listening so hard to it, when everything else inside her urged her toward Ty, not away from him.

"He can sit by us, right, Mom?"

"I like Ty Barker," she said, her voice half an octave too high. "He's a good boy."

"He's not a boy," River muttered, finally sending him the message that he could sit by her family at the picnic. That opened a conversation about his role in helping with the picnics, which he confirmed he'd just signed on for and had forgotten about.

He asked her again if she'd consider helping out, if she wasn't too busy at Silver Creek. She honestly had no idea what her job would require of her, mentally, physically, or emotionally. She already felt drained in so many ways, and without the opportunity to spiritually rejuvenate herself because of Ty's proximity, River leaned her head back and closed her eyes.

"It's okay to like him," her mom said.

River let her head loll to the side and opened her eyes to look out the window. The town rolled by, much the same way River felt like her life currently was sliding by.

"You used to like him," her mom continued.

"I know, Mom."

"What happened?"

River heaved a sigh. "Nothing, Mom. Absolutely nothing

happened." And that, in River's opinion, was the real problem.

CHAPTER 4

*A*fter a nap, and consuming a gallon of diet soda, River found her second wind. Well, at least enough wind to make it to the picnic, her warm cheddar biscuits resting beneath a crisp, white tea towel. Her mother's cake was not covered, and she carried it like it was the crown jewel of picnic foods. She set it on the end of the table housing desserts and was quickly whisked away by the knitting club she'd joined the previous year.

River watched her go, and though she had Lexi and Hannah with her—they were always with her—she felt utterly alone and abandoned. She moved down the table to the bread section and placed her biscuits in an empty spot. She turned, expecting to fumble around socially for a few minutes until the feasting started.

Sure enough, she didn't see anyone she cared to converse with, so she guided her girls away from the food tables and toward the playground. "Go on and play," she said. "I'll call you when it's time to eat."

Lexi and Hannah ran off, and River grinned at their exuberance. She pushed her hands in her jeans pockets and glanced around again.

"I was half-expecting you not to show."

She startled at Ty's deep voice, so close and so comforting. She found him on her left, only inches away. "You've got to stop sidling up to me."

"Sidling?" He laughed, that same boisterous, carefree sound she'd enjoyed as a teen.

"Yes, sidling. You're like a ninja, appearing out of nowhere."

"I'm just standin' here, sweetheart."

The endearment made her heart trip at the same time it tried to rip itself free from her veins. "Sweetheart?" She gave a mirthless laugh. "Don't call me that."

His fingertips glossed down her forearm. "You used to like it when I called you that."

"Then you stopped calling completely." She arched her brow at him and walked away, unsure of why she simultaneously wanted to bring him closer and push him away.

He caught her easily, what with those long legs and all. "I stopped calling because you moved a thousand miles away three weeks after—" He cut off so suddenly she thought he'd been struck mute.

Her heart roared like a lion, and she felt as trapped as a wild animal behind glass, with spectators studying her. "Three weeks after what?" she asked.

"After I kissed you." He glared at her, the edges around his rock-hard eyes crumbling with every passing second. "Must've been a terrible kiss." He smiled, and the wattage on this one could light a dozen Christmas trees. Did he know how beautiful his face was when it was lit up like that? Soft and rugged and handsome at the same time. Her fingers flinched toward his face, as if she'd trace that smile so she could feel it later.

"It wasn't," she managed to push out of her throat.

The smile turned from flirty to foxy in less than a blink. "No?" He touched her again with his calloused fingers, and she wanted to press her palm against his and see if his hand still fit in hers like a missing puzzle piece. "Maybe we should try it again just to make sure."

River's skin tingled where he touched her, and the lion's roar in her heart moved to her bloodstream. *Yes!* her mind screamed. *Yes, we should definitely try again!*

"River?" Katie stepped up to them, creating a triangle and causing Ty to drop his hand. "Hannah needs you." She pointed back the way she'd come, and River found her crying three-year-old easily.

"Excuse me." She ducked her head as she hurried away, grateful and annoyed at the interruption. She needed to figure out how to exist somewhere in the middle of the spectrum, because this constant emotional back and forth wasn't very pleasant.

She glanced over her shoulder, where Ty stood watching her, an intensity in his gaze she could feel from twenty feet away. Katie said something to him, and he focused on her, breaking the spell he'd cast on River. As she bent to lift Hannah into her arms, River reminded herself that she hadn't come home to find a new husband, but to start a new, more stable, life with her girls.

And not the kind of stable where she'd find a handsome cowboy waiting to hold her hand.

———

Ty took a few seconds to explain to Katie what she'd interrupted. She cocked her hip and folded her arms, a look on her face he'd seen before. "Really?" she asked.

"I sort of dated her in high school," he said.

"Yeah, right." Katie glanced back to where River Lee now crouched in front of Hannah. "We grew up together, and I would've known. Plus, she's way out of your league."

"It was a summer fling," Ty said. "And you're totally right about her being out of my league. That's why I need your help."

"Why should I help you?" She narrowed her dark green eyes at him, and he could see so much of Caleb in her. "You dumped me after one dance."

"Katie," he said, pressing his hand over his heart as if she'd hurt him. "I did no such thing. Caleb wouldn't let me ask you out."

"At least one of you has a brain."

"C'mon, Katie." He linked his arm through hers. He *had* asked her to dance, one time, one summer several years ago. Caleb had put a stop to that immediately, which was fine

44

with Ty. Katie was cute, but there was no spark between them. Now River Lee…. There was an entire fireworks show happening inside Ty's chest, and he didn't know what to do with the explosions, the smoke, the heat.

"Just, say something nice about me if she asks," he said.

"She won't ask."

"She won't?"

"She's pretty private."

"Closed off," Ty said, thinking that was a better way of putting it.

"She's divorced," Katie said. "Raising two kids by herself. She's *guarded*."

Mind working overtime, Ty faced Katie. "How long do you think she needs?"

"How long for what?"

He glanced back at River Lee, his desire skyrocketing when he caught her looking at him too. "How long before she's ready to start dating again." Ty focused on Katie again, desperate for a number so he could stop obsessing about when he could ask her out.

"Don't you have a girlfriend?"

Ty grinned. "Nope. Broke up with her at church this morning."

"You are something else." A look of disgust crossed her face a moment before she broke out laughing. "You broke up with a woman at church?"

"It's not like we were really dating. I hadn't even kissed her."

"Oh, is that the measurement you're using? You're not dating a woman until you kiss?"

"Sure," Ty said. "That sounds good."

Katie rolled her eyes and tossed her caramel-colored hair over her shoulder. "Six months, Ty. I think you should give River six more months."

Disappointment blipped through Ty like the rhythm on a heart monitor. *Six-months. Six-six-months?*

Six months seemed like a lifetime to Ty. But he put on a smile he hoped indicated he wouldn't ask River Lee to dinner for six—more—months, and broadcast it at her as she rejoined them, Hannah balanced on her hip. "So I heard your mom brought her cake. Can you help me find that?"

The mask she wore cracked, and a tiny smile slipped through. Ty felt like he'd won the Heisman trophy with the appearance of that smile, it being the first she'd given him since practically trampling him the previous day.

"You better hurry," she said. "Might want to go for dessert first." She nodded toward the tables laden with food, where people had started to line up.

Before he could think, he grabbed her free hand and towed her toward the end of the table covered with desserts. "Which one is it?" He liked the way her hand felt in his, but he tried not to focus on it too much. If he did, everything in his life would slow down, operating as if he were underwater. Except his heart. That raced liked it was fleeing from a predator.

She laughed—really laughed—and nodded toward a tall,

four-layer cake bearing deep, dark chocolate icing and adorned with red frosting roses.

"Get me a piece," River Lee said as Ty searched for a knife, and then a plate. The line of people inched closer, and he really should be helping to make sure the rolls didn't run out, but he sliced and scooped and scampered away with River Lee's giggle searing his eardrums.

Once in the safety of a tall birch tree, he handed the plate to River Lee. "You guard this for me. I have some things to take care of, but when I get back, I'm going to enjoy every bite." Her bright blue eyes sparkled like the sun shining off Caribbean waters, and he got lost for a moment thinking about what he really wanted to taste.

Only his sense of community duty tore him from her—and Katie's warning that River Lee needed six more months before Ty could take her to dinner—and he hurried to the pavilion to see where he was needed. He cut rolls for barbeque sandwiches, and replenished napkins and plates, and cleared away dishes as they emptied. He flashed smiles here and there, but he still felt removed from the people surrounding him. Mostly families or couples, Ty wasn't sure where he belonged. He'd volunteered to see if he could find somewhere or someone to connect to, and he hadn't really done that yet.

He pushed back his frustration in favor of patting a little dog being led by a little girl, and removing the pan that had once held delicious-smelling peach cake squares, and reporting back to the group service leader for his next assignment.

"Go eat," Pearl said, and Ty didn't ask twice. By the time he returned to the shady tree, River Lee leaned against the trunk, both her daughters fast asleep and snuggled into her side.

"Hey." Ty eased to the ground and picked up the hunk of cake she'd left for him. "Nap time?"

"Mm." She let her eyes fall closed as a smile graced her face, the slow, sleepy quality of her the sexiest thing Ty had seen in a long, long time.

"How was the cake?" he asked.

"Fantastic."

"Did you get lunch?" He surveyed the plates littering the ground nearby, with various leftovers.

"My mom brought us sandwiches and chips."

Ty nodded, his stomach roaring for more than chocolate, but as soon as he took a bite of cake, he changed his mind. This was all he needed.

Chocolate and the company of River Lee.

Six months, he thought as he allowed himself to study her while she had her eyes closed. He wasn't even sure he'd been in a relationship for that long, let alone waited that long for something he wanted. Of course, if his sisters were to be believed, that was Ty's biggest problem: impatience. That, and all the girls he dated.

Still, Vienna always said if Ty were a little more patient with the girls he dated, he might've actually found one he could stand to spend his life with. He'd always argued that he knew within the first hour or so if he wanted to spend more time with someone.

Vienna had been married for eight years, and well, Ty wasn't even close to getting married. As he glanced around the park, he realized why this picnic had always held such allure for him. Almost a sense of wonderment.

There were families here. Couples. Very few single men or women. This monthly summer picnic was a life Ty didn't have, a life he'd never even thought he wanted.

His gaze landed back on River Lee and her girls, and something in his life shifted. River Lee hadn't been especially welcoming to him, barely speaking to him at the horseback riding lesson and her house, and only allowing herself to give him one smile in all the time they'd talked over the past couple of days.

But he was willing to be patient—for her.

She opened her eyes at the same moment he scooped the last of the cake into his mouth. "You ate that fast," she said with a playful glimmer in her eyes.

"It's all I've had today." He stood. "I'm gonna go grab some real food. You'll be here when I get back?"

She nodded toward her oldest daughter. "I don't think I'm going anywhere." When she lifted her chin again, a beautiful smile hugged her face. Ty basked in the warmth of it, even if it wasn't for him.

He beat a path back to the food tables, made himself a couple of barbeque pork sandwiches, and snagged an almost-empty bag of sour cream and cheddar potato chips. With a couple cans of soda tucked under his arm, he went back to River Lee's side.

She watched him and he struggled with something to

say, something to ask her. "What are you doing at Silver Creek?" he asked.

"I've got my degree in general counseling," she said. "I'm going to be a therapist there."

"So you aren't one of the counselors who oversees a group of girls."

"I will have eight girls assigned to me, yes," she said. "But no, I'm not the one who'll get them to their activities and such. Those people are called group leaders now."

"I was wrong then," he said. "I think it's the group leaders who have a high turnover." He focused on his food. "Do you like counseling?"

"Sure." She spoke with such a false note, though, that Ty didn't believe her.

He studied her from under the brim of his cowboy hat. "Have you ever been a counselor before?"

Those aqua eyes hardened into gems as brilliant as sapphires. "No, actually, I haven't."

"So you don't know if you like it."

"I spent six years in college doing it." She glared at him with all the ferocity of a mama bear. "I like it just fine."

Ty raised one hand in surrender. He didn't want to argue with her; he just wanted to talk, and she certainly wasn't putting forth any conversation topics.

Thankfully, before Ty could ask another potentially relationship-ruining question—like "Will you go to dinner with me tomorrow night?"—Pearl appeared.

"When you're finished there, would you mind helping

with the trash? Charlie insisted he could do it, but well, he's already replaced one hip."

Ty glanced up into the older woman's face, a kinship forming at the respect in her eyes and the concern for Charlie in his voice. "Sure thing, Pearl."

"Thanks, Ty." She glanced at River Lee. "I don't think we've met."

"Oh." Ty wiped his mouth with his napkin. "Pearl Gregory, this is River Lee Whitely. She's—"

"It's not River Lee Whitely." She threw him an impatient glare. "It's River—no *Lee*—Taylor."

Ty blinked and blanched, his brain sorting information so fast, he couldn't keep up with the exchange in front of him until Pearl said, "Looks like you got your hands full there, but we could always use more help."

"Yes, I know. Ty's invited me to help out with a few things."

"You really should," he said. "It's fun, and it's not hard. You could've helped with this while the girls played."

She cocked her head, amusement running through her expression. "I'm thinking about it."

"You are?" Ty couldn't help the disbelief in his voice.

River Lee rolled her eyes. "Go help that poor old man with the trash before he hurts himself."

Ty grinned, sensing a weak spot in her defenses. "Yes, ma'am." He saluted her and sprang to his feet, making it to the trashcan in the pavilion mere moments before Charlie threw out his back trying to lift an overly full bag.

CHAPTER 5

*I*t's *River—no Lee* taunted Ty for the rest of the evening. He wouldn't see her until next weekend, and that just didn't sit right in his gut.

Yes, he had her phone number, but he didn't dare use it. He stood in front of the mirror in his cabin and said, "River. Riv-River Taylor." There was just so much wrong with that name. It didn't even fit her. She was River Lee, heavy on the twang, her second name almost two syllables by itself.

And how would he have finished that sentence if she hadn't interrupted him? "This is River Lee," he said. "She's my—" He stared into his own eyes, at a complete loss for what River Lee was to him.

If he said a friend, would that be a lie? They'd been friendly that day. Maybe not on Saturday, what with her practically trying to use one of his beloved horses to cause his death.

She certainly wasn't his girlfriend. A wicked smile

curved his lips. "Yet." He turned away from the mirror, a bit of embarrassment slipping through him for his personal pep talk. If Caleb had witnessed such a thing, Ty would never hear the end of it.

But Caleb lived with Holly now, just a couple cabins down. Ty had never been a jealous man, but something strange coated the back of his throat when he thought of Caleb and Holly. When he remembered how shocked he'd been to realize all the girls at the summer dances were so much younger than him. It was like he'd aged and hadn't realized it.

He had never minded dating girls in their early twenties, but now that he'd turned thirty, he felt a bit squicky about it. Problem was, there weren't that many women more his age in Gold Valley. And Ty had been looking.

"Always looking," he muttered to himself as he grabbed a frozen burrito and stuck it in the microwave. Caleb would be horrified—he put together the most random ingredients to make things like tuna fish sandwiches with potato chips and tomatoes, or scrambled eggs with everything but the kitchen sink mixed in.

Ty was more of a food purist, plus he was useless in the kitchen. Useless with laundry too—he actually hired his out after he'd turned all his socks and underwear pink. And he'd had to invest in new socks and underwear. It was actually cheaper to pay for the laundry service than it was to replace the clothes he ruined.

He slathered sour cream on the burrito and ate it, the walls of his cabin pressing ever closer. He needed to get outside, get on his horse, and get up the mountain. Once free of the cabin, Ty finally breathed. He went through the motions of saddling his personal horse, Abracadabra, his fingers doing the work but his mind circling River Lee and if he could really hang on for six months without asking her out.

He'd already touched her, and she hadn't jerked away like she loathed the feel of his skin against hers. And the flirting with giving the kiss another try...he probably needed to stuff talk like that down his throat and keep it there.

The mountains surrounding Gold Valley had always enthralled Ty. He loved getting on his horse's back and going steadily up. Up to check the herd. Up to plant the crops. Up to harvest. Up to the remote cabins the cowboys used when they did their chores on the mountain. Just up, and away from his life, his worries, his concerns.

And honestly, Ty didn't have a lot of those anyway. As Abra clomped steadily up the hill, the tension in Ty's shoulders waned. He whistled a tune his grandpa used to sing while he whittled in the tool shed, Ty's absolute favorite place as a boy.

So he didn't quite fit in with Caleb and Jace anymore. So they'd gotten married, and Jace had a son now. Big deal. Ty was still healthy, still happy, and still honest. He'd never given much thought to marrying, especially because dating and experimenting with different girls every so often was fun.

When he'd told Vienna he liked dating a lot of girls, she'd

rolled her eyes and told him to "get serious." And, well, Ty liked dancing through life. If he didn't care about something, he wouldn't be disappointed when he didn't get it.

Still, his heart kept tripping around River Lee, and he wondered if he'd change the tune to which he was dancing if she'd step in and tango with him.

———

By the end of the week, River felt like she'd been run over by ten horses. The aches in her back had been amplified by the bendy way she'd let Lexi and Hannah sleep on her at the picnic on Sunday. Coupled with her natural hunched position at her desk for the past week, and River needed to get outside, stretch out, and then find time to catch a nap.

But she had no time for napping, she knew. With horseback riding lessons in the morning, River wouldn't even get a break on the weekend. Moms never did get a break, she supposed.

Her mind landed on Ty, as it had been doing all week. At first, she'd pushed him out as soon as he appeared, but as the days wore on and her traitorous brain kept bringing him to the forefront, she'd entertained a few ideas about him.

Ideas about holding his hand. Her fingers trembled.

Ideas about serving with him on the community events. Her throat turned dry.

Ideas about kissing him. Her heart thumped.

It was about this point that she shut the fantasies off,

cleared her throat as if those in the nearby vicinity would know what she'd been thinking about, and refocused on her tasks.

With him so ingrained in her psyche, she had done something she hoped would cure her: She'd called Pearl Gregory and volunteered to help with the town's Harvest Days festivities. A week-long affair in the middle of August, Harvest Days had been running in Gold Valley for over a century.

As a child and teen, River had enjoyed the parade, the carnival, the fun run, the tennis tournaments, all of it. Several of the events had changed, and the committee was meeting for just a "quick half hour" according to Pearl to get some assignments made before too many more days passed.

River's pulse beat a frantic rhythm against the back of her tongue. She wasn't sure if Ty would be at the meeting or not, and she hadn't had the courage to ask Pearl about him specifically. No need to get people talking when there was nothing to talk about.

Plus, it was a long drive up the canyon to Horseshoe Home Ranch, and surely he couldn't jaunt down every time there was a quick meeting. Still, as she pulled into the community center's parking lot, the muscles in her body quivered in anticipation of seeing him.

Why, she wasn't sure. It wasn't like she was going to touch him. An echo of his fingertips running down her arm made her shiver, and she shook her head. "Get ahold of yourself," she whispered furiously as she entered the building.

A long counter ran along her right, and she stepped up to the receptionist there. "I'm looking for the Harvest Days planning meeting?"

The woman smiled. "It's in room one hundred. Down the hall toward the pool, on your right."

River's eyebrows arched up. Pool? Since when did Gold Valley have an indoor pool? *Since you left, thirteen years ago,* River told herself as she walked down the hall. Her low heels made clicking sounds against the painted concrete, and she found room one hundred easily enough.

She slowed as she approached, popping her head into the room to see if she was the first to arrive. She had left Silver Creek a little early, not able to sit at her desk for one more minute. Counseling was much harder than she'd anticipated, especially with troubled girls who didn't want to talk.

She was not the first one there.

Dreamy, dark, and delicious Ty Barker sat at the table, and his eyes drank her in when he saw her. "Well, hello there," he said, every syllable coated in pure Montana cowboy country twang.

River had no choice but to enter the room, which she wanted to do anyway. She schooled her face into what she hoped was an impassive expression as she walked toward him. "Hello yourself."

"What are you doin' here?"

She took a seat next to him, lifted her chin, and sniffed. "I volunteered."

A soft scoff escaped his throat, causing her gaze to shoot

in his direction. "You volunteered." He wasn't asking, and he looked genuinely shocked, like she'd just told him Santa delivered presents from Mars instead of the North Pole.

"I used to love Harvest Days when I was a kid," she said by way of explanation. She certainly couldn't tell him she'd volunteered so she could see him more often. Oh, no. That secret was going to the grave with her.

"It's not the same as when we were kids," Ty said.

"No?" River bent to pull a notepad out of her purse. "What's different?"

"Lots of stuff," he said.

"There's still a parade, right?"

"The main one on Saturday morning, yes. And the children's one is on Wednesday afternoon."

"Do the kids still get free rodeo tickets if they participate in the parade?"

"Yep."

"Lots the same then." She tossed her curled hair over her shoulder and wrote the date at the top of her notebook.

Ty chuckled, the sexy sound causing every defense River had put in place to crumble into dust. The man really was dangerous to her health. *Why* had she volunteered?

She closed her eyes and offered up a prayer for guidance, for peace. She'd volunteered so she could see more of Ty. And here she was, seeing him. Would it be so terrible if he wanted to see more of her too?

Her ex, John, had already moved on. She'd seen pictures of him and his secretary splashed all over social media. He hadn't done it maliciously, but it still hurt. River had stayed in Nevada until the court had settled on the custody of Lexi and Hannah, and then she'd left. It was too hard to stay in Las Vegas, too hard to think of the friends she'd lost, of John's two sisters who used to be like sisters to River and now wouldn't talk to her.

Not only that, but Lexi and Hannah had lost their aunts. His parents had still been interested, but they'd understood when she'd called to tell them she was moving back to Montana. She'd promised pictures and cards.

She wiped the memories from her mind as another man entered the room, followed closely by Pearl. This was a business meeting. She could be professional. If Ty wanted to grab something to eat after, well, River needed dinner as much as the next person and there was no crime in sharing a meal with a friend.

By the time the "quick half hour" meeting had reached an hour, River had realized how true Ty had spoken. A lot had changed about Harvest Days. There was an entire Huck Finn fishing event to plan—which she'd signed up for because it was in the afternoon, and her counseling caseload was easier in the afternoons.

Ty had immediately volunteered to help her with the event, a glint in his eye that made rockets zoom through her veins.

There was a pickleball tournament to organize. A 5K run to advertise, get permits for, and begin registration for. The main parade had it's own committee, as did the carnival, but Ty served on that one, so River added her name to it as well.

She didn't dare look at him as she did, because she wasn't sure she'd be able to keep her true feelings hidden.

"One more thing," Pearl said. "Who can work with the church to make sure we have enough volunteers for the concessions at the rodeo?" She looked up expectantly from a large binder she'd brought with her. "Its just emails and phone calls, mostly. The pastor and his community outreach coordinator usually do it all, actually."

"I can," River said. "All I have is the Huck Finn Day and help with the carnival."

"The carnival is big," Pearl said. "That requires permits and road closures too."

River swallowed, thinking maybe she'd bitten off more than she could chew simply by coming to the meeting. "I go to church anyway. I can talk to the pastor."

"Sydnee is the community outreach coordinator," Ty said, like River should know who that was.

"Sydnee?" she asked.

"Yeah, you know." He leaned back in his chair and folded his arms. "Sydnee Hatter? She played softball. Graduated the same year as you."

Recollection flooded River's mind. "Oh, Sydnee, right. I can contact her."

"I'll help with that too," Ty said.

"You have enough," Pearl said.

"And River Lee—uh." He cut her a look filled with apology and panic. "*River* can do most of the heavy lifting on this one. But she'll need help organizing all the volunteers. It's four nights of people. It's a lot."

Warmth bloomed beneath River's breastbone. He'd made an attempt to call her the right name. She ducked her head as a smile stole across her face. A smile she couldn't contain in a box, or behind a door, or beneath a rock. A smile she almost wanted Ty to see.

The meeting ended, and she stuffed her notepad in her purse, shouldered the bag, and stood. "Wow," she said. "You weren't kidding when you said they needed more help." Even though there had been a dozen people in the meeting, River was sure they couldn't pull off Harvest Days, which was only two months away.

"More will come," he said. "This was just the initial meeting to get everything cemented." He stepped toward the door, his hands shoved deep into his front pockets.

"Too bad they got rid of the baby contest," she said.

"It was totally lame," Ty said. "Every single baby who was entered won. There were like seven trucks in the parade, all of them hunkered down under umbrellas. You couldn't even *see* the babies."

River laughed, her first reaction. And it felt good, freeing, to laugh like that. She couldn't remember the last time she'd laugh so spontaneously. She stepped wide, almost colliding with Ty. Without thinking too hard about what she was doing, she linked her hand through his elbow. "So, are you staying down in the valley tonight? Or do you have to get back up to the ranch?"

He dipped his face to glance at her, then re-centered his eyes down the hall. "Going back to the ranch. I do the early morning chores on weekends."

"Every weekend?"

"Yeah." He yawned as if the thought of doing the early morning chores made him tired. "That way I can come down to the valley in the afternoons. I have the riding lessons, events, the dances, church…." He let his voice trail off, and River didn't know how to fill the silence between them.

They approached the exit, and she panicked, thinking as soon as they stepped outside, he'd vanish. Vanish into his truck to find dinner on his own. Vanish back up the canyon, where he was so far out of her reach.

"Are you hungry?" she blurted out.

Ty slowed, his footsteps coming to a complete stop. "Am I hungry? Is that a real question?"

She searched his face for some sign of teasing. With Ty, there was always sarcasm and good humor. Some had labeled him a prankster in high school, but River had seen the more serious, more sensitive guy beneath the carefree demeanor. Once. She'd seen him once. And she'd liked him.

"Well, are you?" she asked. "Because I was thinking we could—"

He lifted his finger and placed it against her lips, effectively silencing her and causing a bolt of heat to rebound through her body.

"Just a sec," he whispered. "We?"

Two women came around the corner, obviously having just worked out. Several more committee members were moving toward them too. And there stood Ty, all statuesque, with his thumb practically stroking her bottom lip.

She turned and left the building, the merry-go-round containing her emotions spinning spinning spinning.

"River Lee!" Ty called as he followed her.

She didn't have the energy to correct him on her name. Besides, she actually kind of liked the way it sounded in his voice.

He caught up to her. Of course he did. "I'm always hungry," he said. "You know they don't feed cowboys much out on ranches? We have to make our own dinners."

"What a tragedy." She added an eyeroll to the statement. She fished her keys out of her purse, but Ty snatched them from her fingers. "Ty," she warned.

"*I'll* drive *us* to dinner," he said. "And my truck's over there." He changed direction on a dime, his stride long and powerful and leaving her to rush to catch him. He grinned like he'd won the lottery as he held open the passenger door to his dirty, beat-up ranch truck, and River allowed herself to return the gesture.

But with her heart tap dancing as Ty circled the truck and climbed in the driver's seat, River wondered what in the blazes she was doing.

"Where do you want to go?" he asked.

"Somewhere fast and easy," she said, suddenly thinking of her girls at home.

"Fast and easy." Ty started the truck. "I don't think that describes you at all."

She wasn't sure if she should be horrified by his statement, chastise him, or laugh. She blinked; he grinned wolfishly; she tipped her head back and laughed. He joined her, and it was the sweetest chorus to River's ears.

When she quieted, she said, "Well, at least we got that out of the way. Anything with me is going to be long and hard."

Ty pulled into the street and headed west toward downtown Gold Valley. "That's okay, sweetheart," he said. "I like a challenge. And no one's ever called me a quitter."

CHAPTER 6

*R*iver basked in the air conditioning in Ty's truck, surprised the ancient beast was so well equipped. The radio warbled out an old country song, and Ty hummed along with it. Sweet contentment cascaded through her, and River found herself combing her fingers through her hair and singing the lyrics under her breath.

"Do you like tacos?" Ty asked.

River glanced out the windshield at the row of shops along Main Street. "I like pizza more."

"Pizza is the king of fast and easy." He grinned, and River almost lost consciousness with the dazzling quality of his grin. The man must practice for hours in front of a mirror to get such a quick gesture so perfect. He pulled into the parking lot as he asked, "What do you like on your pizza?"

"Pepperoni," she said. "I'm a purist."

He cocked his chin toward her, his eyes barely slanting

toward her before flitting away. "A purist, huh? So that means nothing but pepperoni."

"Extra cheese?"

Ty parked and killed the engine—and thus the air conditioning. He turned toward her and leaned one arm on the steering wheel. "You should try pepperoni and olives. It's the perfect pairing."

"Something I've never done before," she said, everything in her trying to figure out how to flirt. "Sounds dangerous."

With the twinkle in his eye, River felt like maybe she'd achieved a new high score in the flirtation game.

"We can do half and half," he said. "But we can't sit here without the AC." He pushed open his door and practically leapt from the truck. River barely had her seatbelt unbuckled before he yanked her door open. He reached up to her, and she focused on his hand.

Large, and tan, and calloused, he had the hands of a working man. Excitement tripped through her as she pressed her palm against his. She glanced around, but it was still early for the Friday night dinner crowd, and the street wasn't very busy.

She met his gaze, and even through the shade created by the brim of his hat, she saw a flicker of frustration. Maybe disappointment? Anger? He blinked and the emotion went out. "Shall *we*?"

River rolled her eyes. "I'm never going to live that down, am I?"

Ty nudged her with his elbow but kept her hand

cemented in his. "Oh, sure you will, sweetheart. I rather like the sound of *we* comin' from you."

"You're just going to make me pay for it."

Ty slowed, and River sensed there was more to him than mega-watt smiles, a way with horses, and quick wit. Of course there was. She'd glimpsed it that one summer years ago. Again when he'd helped her mom with the outdoor faucet. A third time when he ran around the picnic to make sure everyone got fed before he even took a single bite.

"River Lee," he drawled, and she decided not to correct him though her spine did stiffen the slightest bit.

"Yes?"

"Are you—I mean." He exhaled and his hand fell away from hers. The loss of it felt colder than River thought possible. "I don't mean to start somethin' you're not ready for."

She wasn't sure how to answer. Ty's desire rode right there in the words he'd said, the space between them, the heated glances in her direction.

"Who says I'm not ready?"

"Katie."

River groaned. "Maybe Katie should keep her mouth shut." She reached for Ty and secured his hand in hers. "I'm starving, I know that. Can we just go eat and not make a national event out of it?"

———

Ty liked the weight of River's hand in his. He liked the way her fingers fit between his. He liked the presence of her beside him, that tantalizing lilac scent teasing him, driving him wild.

"No national events," he said. "Its just pizza."

"Exactly." River Lee stepped toward the pizza joint, towing Ty with her. Not that she had to try that hard. He'd gladly go where she wanted if she'd keep saying *we* and holding his hand. He did notice that she hadn't answered his implied question as to whether she was ready to start a relationship with him or not.

A skin of unease settled over him, but he pushed it back. She was with him, holding his hand. And she'd suggested dinner, not him.

Maybe just follow her lead, he told himself. He hardly ever let someone else lead, and it felt nice to let River Lee step up to the cash register and order a half pepperoni, half pepperoni and olive pizza.

"And sodas," Ty added.

River Lee made a face and shook her head. "Water for me."

"Water?" Ty scoffed and squeezed her hand. "You can have water at home."

"I can make pepperoni pizza at home too."

"Not like this."

She grinned and giggled. "No, definitely not like this." She released his hand to fumble for her purse, but Ty wasn't having any of that. He whipped his wallet out of his back pocket and had his debit card out before she'd even taken another breath.

"Ty," she protested.

"River Lee," he said back, drawing out her second name in a way that would surely annoy her. It did, if the flattened lips and stormy eyes were any indication.

He chuckled. "C'mon." He swept his arm around her waist and tucked her into his side. "Did you really think we were gonna go to dinner and I wouldn't pay?"

"I didn't intend for you to pay when I suggested dinner."

"I know you didn't." Ty stepped away and took his card back, tucking it into his wallet with extra care, trying to take a breath that wasn't full of River Lee's coconut-scented shampoo. He needed to tame the tidal wave of desire threatening to drown him, and touching her wasn't helping with that.

He took his cup over to the soda machine, glad when she went to find a table instead of joining him. *Deep breaths*, he coached himself as he filled the cup with ice and then diet cola. *This is not a date. Not a date. Not a date.*

Just because he'd paid didn't mean it was a date. Just because they sat across from each other in a booth didn't make this a date.

Please help me to say the right things this time, he prayed as he lidded his soda and turned to join her. When he made it to the booth, she lifted her water cup and added a smile to the gesture.

He set his soda down and went to get her drink. "Lemon?" he called over his shoulder. The only other couple in the restaurant had about fifty years on Ty, and they didn't look up from their early dinner.

"Ew. No."

"No lemon," Ty muttered. Nearly every woman he'd dated in the last year wouldn't drink water without lemon in it. Like it was a fashion statement or something. The fact that River Lee didn't like it only set her further apart from the crowd he'd once liked.

He returned to the table and sat down, his breath whooshing out of him.

"Rough week?" she asked.

He gave her a tired smile. "About normal."

She sipped her water, those cerulean eyes never leaving his. "The ranch keeps you busy."

"Always."

"Why do you do the community service then?"

Ty shrugged, not wanting to get into his reasons why, not tonight. He had a hard time articulating them in a way that didn't sound pathetic. "Why did you?"

"Truthfully?"

"Sure, we can be truthful with each other."

"Wanted to see the great Ty Barker in action." The flash of her smile almost blinded him.

"Okay, we've reached the ridiculous part of the evening."

"Is it evening?" She glanced around and leaned toward him. "I don't think four o'clock counts as evening." Her hushed tone and playful manner only increased his desire to see her everyday, talk to her everyday, kiss her everyday.

He agreed, but he'd seen the way she'd glanced around

outside. Like she was looking to make sure no one was around to see her holding his hand. He wasn't sure if he should be offended by her action or try to be understanding. She *had* just gotten back into town, divorced with two little girls. He'd gone with understanding, though there was still a spot somewhere in his chest that pinched.

"How was your week?" he asked. "New job and all."

She settled back into the booth, putting a couple extra feet between them. "It's hard starting a new job. Leaving the girls." Her voice drifted into silence and her gaze wandered out the window.

"Your mom's watching them, right?" Ty sucked down his soda, his stomach suddenly in knots for some reason he couldn't quite name.

"Yes. She retired last year, so she's home. She loves having us here."

"I'm sure she does." Ty wanted to get her attention back, make her stop talking in that low, unhappy voice. But he asked, "Was it hard coming home?" anyway.

She nodded, her focus still on something beyond the pizzeria. "I needed to, and I'd been planning it for months. But it was still hard, yes."

"How long have you been divorced?" Ty cursed himself the moment the words left his mouth. But he hadn't heard from Katie, and no one on the ranch even knew who River Lee was, except maybe Caleb, and well, Ty and Caleb didn't discuss women the way they used to.

River Lee snapped back to the present, and her eyes

blazed with blue fire for one, two, three heartbeats before she relaxed. "This is why I don't go to dinner," she said.

Ty held her gaze. "Why don't you go to dinner?"

"Because then I have to talk." She glanced away, her fingers tumbling over each other, revealing her nerves.

"We can talk about me," Ty offered, though the thought didn't exactly bring him any peace. "What do you want to know?"

She slid him a knowing look through narrowed eyes. "I already know a lot about you."

"Oh yeah?" He leaned his elbows on the table. "Enlighten me."

She straightened and shook her hair over her shoulders. "Okay, well, you work at Horseshoe Home Ranch."

"So far, so good."

"You give horseback riding lessons on the weekends."

He waved his hand for her to go on, wondering when his life had been deduced to two simple sentences. A family of snakes started to writhe in his gut at the thought of what she'd say next. After all, his life *was* the ranch and horseback riding lessons at Silver Creek.

"You do a lot of community service." A glorious blush entered her face, and the corners of Ty's mouth twitched upward.

"I just started last year," he said. "And I am doing a lot more this summer."

"Nothing in the winter?"

He shook his head. "It's too hard to get down the canyon if the weather is bad. I seem to make it to the Christmas

Festival of Trees, though, so I probably could." Ty considered it seriously. He'd been enjoying his service around Gold Valley, the different people he met, the sense of fulfillment he got that he couldn't seem to get anywhere else.

"I think you do enough," River Lee said.

"So that's what you know about me?" Ty asked. "Anyone with two eyes would know that."

She watched him for a few seconds, more thoughts clearly dancing behind her eyes. "I know you've dated every available woman in Gold Valley."

He shook his head. "That's not true."

"It's not?"

"Every available woman?" He scoffed. "Surely no one's done that."

She lifted her water to her lips and sipped. "Was that your goal?"

He shrugged. "Not really. I like dancing and having a good time."

"A good time?" Her eyebrows went up, along with the pitch of her voice.

"Nothing serious." He reached for his soda and gulped, the carbonation burning his throat on the way down.

"So you're not looking for a serious relationship?"

"Depends."

"On what?"

"On who it's with." He cocked one eyebrow in her direction, his meaning crystal clear to him. He hoped to her too. By the deepening stain in her face, Ty was pretty sure his message had gotten through, loud and clear.

She cleared her throat at the same time the waiter arrived with their pizza. *Saved by pepperoni,* Ty thought as he grinned up at the guy and thanked him. He steered the conversation toward her girls after that, and River Lee came alive talking about them. Ty satisfied himself with the food and the pretty little sound of her voice.

Something seethed inside him, though. Something that spoke of how much she adored her children—and if she even had room for him in her life.

CHAPTER 7

The next morning, Ty arrived at Silver Creek in a foul mood. Such things were rare for him, as he could usually shrug off whatever was bothering him after a cup of coffee and a maple bar from the best bakery in the world, The Dough Boy on Main Street in Gold Valley. But he'd had his maple bar *and* a cinnamon twist and *two* cups of coffee and he still didn't feel like talking to anyone.

But talk he would have to.

Perpetually early, Ty had twenty minutes before he expected anyone else to show up, so he wandered down the aisle in the horse barn, his fingers finding the soft hair on each horse's nose as he murmured sweet nothings to them. "You guys ready for today?" he asked. "Gotta be patient with the people. They're new to this riding thing."

Kimchi snuffled, and Ty smiled, suddenly all his negativity gone. He hadn't meant to get so wrapped up in River Lee so fast. At the same time, he wasn't sure how to go slower. Everything about her made him want to jam both feet on the accelerator.

And then there was the spiral he'd fallen into last night. He felt like a complete jerk for wondering if she had room for him in her life. Her kids should come first, he knew that. But the selfish side of him wanted to be number one in her life.

And you'll never be number one, he thought for at least the fiftieth time. He breathed deep and scratched Kimchi's neck. "That's okay, though, right?" He gazed at the horse's long nose, her dark eyes. "I don't mean to be selfish."

He'd prayed for what felt like a long time last night for the selfish feelings to go away. They hadn't, and they still circled like sharks this morning. He moved down the row of horses to Pompeii, the huge horse River Lee had tried to tame by herself. A chuckle worked its way loose from the back of his throat, and Pompeii nosed his shoulder as if to say, *Don't be laughing at me. Where's the hay cubes?*

"I brought apples today, guys," he said in a louder voice. "You gotta work hard and be patient, and then you'll get one."

He'd barely twisted back to offer Pompeii a proper scratch when a woman said, "Do you always show up early and talk to the horses?"

River Lee. A smile bloomed on Ty's face and he touched his forehead to Pompeii's before turning, offering a silent prayer of thanks to the Lord for the way her voice could erase the clouds in his soul.

He wondered what that meant, what that said about

their relationship, but he pushed the heavy question to the back of his mind where he could study it out later.

"Mornin'." He turned toward her and leaned against Pompeii's gate, one hand still stroking the horse's neck. "You're early too. Thinkin' you might trample me again?"

She rolled her eyes though the faintest of smiles adorned her face. "I didn't trample you."

He scanned her in her slim-cut jeans and violet top, which hugged her shoulders and left her arms bare. She wore cowgirl boots and her white-blonde hair back in a ponytail, exposing her slender neck and high cheekbones. He swallowed when he realized he was staring, and staring hard.

"You didn't answer my question." She stepped toward him, giving the horses on her left a wide berth.

Ty turned back to Pompeii and tried to steal some of the horse's calm energy. He still felt like someone had unleashed the Tasmanian devil inside his chest when he said, "Yeah, I like talkin' to the horses."

"Why?" She slipped into place next to him. "They don't talk back."

"And that's a beautiful thing," he said. "You can tell them anything, and they don't judge you. They don't tell you you're wrong, or you should've done something different with your life. They don't say you're impatient, or that—" Ty cut off when he realized what was streaming from his mouth. "And," he added in a brighter tone. "They don't tell your secrets to anyone else." He felt the weight of River

Lee's gaze on his face, but he kept beaming up at Pompeii, his heart a piece of cement beneath his ribs.

Why had he said all that? Maybe she—

"Do you want to do something different with your life?" she asked, dashing his hopes that she'd just let his soliloquy slide.

"No."

"What are you wrong about?"

He cut her a glance out of the corner of his eye. "Lots of things. Let's get started." He hurried away, toward the tack room, nervous about where the conversation would lead. He wasn't unhappy with his life, and he didn't make a lot of mistakes. But Vienna's words, though a year old, had cropped up in his life, filled with venom.

Maybe he was too impatient when it came to women. Maybe he was just dancing through life, not taking anything seriously. He took his job seriously; he took the lessons seriously.

As he lifted two saddles, he wondered if he could take a relationship with River Lee as seriously as he needed to.

———

River's back hurt after five minutes on Ole Red, the same horse she'd ridden last week. He plodded along like he'd lost half the batteries he needed to operate, but she still felt one breath away from falling.

"You're squeezin' him too tight," Ty said as she rounded

the corner and came back toward him. "You don't drive the horse with your legs, River Lee."

She gave him a curt nod but couldn't seem to make her thighs relax. The way he drawled out her name didn't help the rate of her pulse, and she almost lost her focus right then and there. The humiliation of falling off a horse right in front of the most gorgeous man on earth was enough to keep her in the saddle—but her legs squeezed even tighter.

"River Lee!" he called, not a note of frustration in his voice. "Relax!"

I can't! she wanted to scream. She needed a new instructor if she was to relax. As he switched his attention to the rider behind her, the tension drained out of River's body. Ole Red lifted his head and seemed to walk with more bounce in his step, and somehow his good energy calmed her further.

Her muscles spasmed the closer she got to Ty again, and she wouldn't allow herself to look in his direction.

"Come over here." He swept the reins right out of her hand, and guided Ole Red to the fence line. "He can feel your tension." Ty stepped onto the bottom rung of the fence, and before she knew it, he'd swung himself into the saddle behind her. His breath tickled the back of her neck and his words dripped like honey through her hair. "You have to be relaxed."

Ty lifted the reins over her head, his strong arms coming around her. He held the lines in one hand and pushed gently with the other against her shoulder. "Relax, River Lee." His voice sounded like a heavenly chorus, and warmth poured through her at his touch. When her back met his very solid chest, a display of fireworks danced through her vision.

She could definitely get used to relaxing in his arms. Her body turned soft and she allowed herself to melt into him. She had no choice really. At this point, her body was acting of its own accord.

"There you go," he said, the husky quality of his voice further lulling her into a sense of safety and peace. "You hold the reins now." He transferred them to her and put his hands on the saddle horn in front of her. "Tell 'im to go left by inching that side back. There's nothing to be done with the legs. They hold you on, that's it."

She eased back on the left rein and Ole Red obeyed easily. Ty could've sat up straighter, she was sure. He didn't need to keep his mouth so close to her ear, she knew. Without him behind her, as relaxed as she was, she suspected she'd fall right off this animal.

River glanced around and found at least three pairs of eyes on her and Ty, which caused an internal alarm to sound and all her muscles to seize. Instantly, Ty took the reins, moved Ole Red closer to the fence, and dismounted.

"You try it alone," he said, handing the reins back without making eye contact. "Go on. Circle around." He moved back to his position on the far end of the circle, already giving directions to a group leader about holding the reins too tight.

River scraped her hand across her forehead, the sweat

there not only because of the summer sun. She still felt like the very sky had eyes on her, and she couldn't shake the feeling for the rest of the session.

Afterward, she participated in the horse care lesson and took the time to brush down Ole Red, feed him the apple he'd been promised, and put him back in his stall. By the time she finished, only she, Ty, and one group leader remained. Ty made sure everything was done, then locked up the barn and headed toward the parking lot with them.

River wanted to invite him to her mother's for lunch, but the courage she needed to speak didn't come.

"See you next week," the group leader said to him, and River seized onto those words and repeated them.

Ty lifted his hand in a general wave and climbed in his truck. He didn't look at her, didn't hesitate before starting the vehicle and driving away. River couldn't help feeling a bit abandoned, and she didn't even know why. Did she really think he'd spend the whole day with her?

He had a family in the valley too, and probably preparations for the dance that night. They hadn't discussed spending any time together today, even if he had held her hand after dinner the previous night. Even if he had leaned into the doorway of her truck back at the community center, given her that bone-melting grin, and said, "I had a great time, River Lee."

She could've subsisted on those words for weeks, no food or water necessary. But when he'd added, "I hope *we* can get together again soon," her heart had floated right up to the clouds.

River shook the sting of his departure away. Hannah and Lexi were expecting croissant sandwiches from the deli for lunch, and River didn't want to be late. Still, she couldn't help thinking that it wouldn't be hard to pick up one more sandwich and have one more person eating in the backyard with them that day.

She started her car and sat in it as the group leader pulled out. She stared through the windshield to the road in front of her, and the mountain just on the other side. The birch trees were beautiful, their green leaves and white trunks something she'd definitely missed in Vegas. Up the mountain to the right sat the exclusive cabin community, where she'd gone to exactly one party in high school.

Gold Valley spread out on her left, sandwiched between two glorious peaks, the northern one still capped with snow, even halfway through June. It wasn't a crossroads, not really. But River felt pulled in several directions.

She hadn't come home to find a man to share her life with, but did that mean she couldn't? Shouldn't?

She had two little girls to care for, but did that mean she had to do it alone?

What do you want?

The question entered her mind, almost from an other-worldly source. She closed her eyes and tipped her head back. "I want to do what's right for me, Lexi, and Hannah." Tears pricked behind her eyes, heating her face despite the air conditioning blowing. "What's right for me, Lexi, and Hannah?"

God didn't answer with the sound of a drum, or a crash

of thunder, or anything loud at all. A simple feeling came into her heart; a feeling that she was loved.

Not an answer, but something. She let the tears fall for a moment, grateful for the reassurance from on high. Then she opened her eyes, wiped her face, and reached for her phone.

CHAPTER 8

*R*iver waited impatiently while the line rang, hoping Katie wasn't with a client. But it was Saturday, and the salon was always booked on the weekend.

Finally, Katie said, "Hey, River."

Relief washed through River, and she wasn't even sure why. She didn't want to talk to her mom about Ty, not yet, because her mother obviously had a soft spot for the man already.

"Katie," River said. "Are you busy?"

"I have a couple of minutes."

"Great." River drew in a deep breath. "I want to talk about Ty Barker."

Katie giggled. "Oh, honey, that's gonna take longer than a couple of minutes."

She thought of him driving away, and panic pounced through her that he'd stop for lunch before she could invite him to her mother's. Maybe she should've called him first.

"We went to dinner last night," River said.

"Ooh," Katie squealed. "And?"

"And nothing. It was nice."

"And?" Katie asked again.

"And...I don't know."

"Did he kiss you?"

"Katie," River admonished. "Of course not. It was dinner at four o'clock in the afternoon."

"Was it a date?"

"I—I don't know." River had been out of the dating game for so long, she wasn't sure what counted as a date and what didn't. Especially for Ty Barker, the ladies' man of Gold Valley.

"Well, it probably wasn't a date," Katie said. "Ty told me he doesn't consider himself dating a woman until he kisses her."

"He—" River paused, her mind trying to latch on to what Katie had said. "What?" Hurt seeped through her. "So he could go to dinner with another woman," she said. "And that would be okay, because he's not dating anyone right now."

"According to his rules," Katie said. "My next client just showed up. I have to go."

"Bye," River said, her voice hollow and robotic. "Don't be stupid," she told herself as she flipped her car into gear and turned toward the valley. "Of course you're not dating just because he bought pizza one time."

She eyed her phone, sitting there in the console, taunting her to just call Ty and invite him to lunch. It wasn't a date if her mother was there, was it?

"Apparently it's not a date until he kisses you," she muttered, not quite sure how she felt about his rule. Not quite sure how she felt about *him*. But quite sure she wanted to find out, even if it took a while. After all, he'd said he liked a challenge, that he wasn't a quitter. Well, she did too, and the only thing she'd ever quit was her marriage because her husband had decided he liked his secretary more than his wife.

She pulled the car to the side of the road and snatched the phone from the console. She had Ty's number dialed before she could second-guess herself.

———

Ty sat in his truck, alone at the drive-in. His mother would make dinner, but she never made lunch, and after a morning of near-disastrous horseback riding lessons, Ty needed nourishment. His phone rang, and he glanced at it, choking at the name on the screen of his phone. *River Lee.*

He thought for sure he'd just thrown his chance at a relationship with her down the drain when he'd climbed on that horse behind her.

Answer it, his mind screamed at him. *Answer it before she hangs up!*

He swiped on the call at the same time he swallowed the bite of hamburger he had in his mouth. "Hello?" Maybe she'd dropped her phone and someone else had picked it up.

"Ty, hey."

Definitely her voice. "River Lee?"

"Are you surprised it's me? Doesn't your phone tell you who's calling?"

"Yeah, and...yeah."

She huffed into the phone, but he didn't offer anything else. *She* was the one embarrassed to be seen with him. He'd felt her relax all the way against him on that horse, and he wanted to hold her like that every day, whisper in her ear all kinds of things, smell the coconut of her shampoo as he lathered her hair in the shower.

He pulled back on his fantasies, putting a tight leash on them so they didn't infect him more than they already had.

Because he'd also witnessed her glancing around, stiffening when she realized how many people were watching them, putting off a cold vibe at his proximity.

"I promised Lexi and Hannah sandwiches for lunch," she said. "I was wondering...well, I was...I thought maybe you'd like one too."

Ty glanced at the bag of food on the seat next to him. "I like sandwiches."

"What kind?"

"Are you going to the sandwich shop or the deli?"

"The deli. Should I go to the sandwich shop?"

"No, the deli is way better." Part butcher, part lunch and dinner station, Ty much preferred the sandwiches at the deli. Paul sliced the meat fresh, and he spent mornings carving meat and making homemade bread. "I like the roast beef with avocado and sprouts at the deli. It's called the Hulk."

"The Hulk, got it."

"Full size," he said, though he'd just eaten half of a combo meal. He didn't much care if he ate at all; he'd be spending time with River Lee.

And her kids, his mind whispered, and Ty acknowledged himself. Of course her kids. He couldn't expect her to leave them with her mom on the weekends too.

"I can swing by the store and get something to drink," he offered. "What do Hannah and Lexi like?"

"That would be great. Thanks, Ty. Let's see, Hannah's favorite is ginger ale, and Lexi likes those lemon-lime sports drinks."

"And you?" he asked. "And don't say water."

She laughed, and Ty thought maybe his blunder would be forgiven. "I don't know what to say now."

"Chocolate milk?" he suggested. "Lemonade?"

"Oh, yeah, do they still have that mango lemonade at the grocery store?"

"In those glass bottles, yeah. I'll get you one." He'd get her a whole case if she'd let him hold her again. "See you soon."

After swinging by the grocery store and getting the drinks, he parked in front of her mother's house, his stomach rioting against the fast food he'd already eaten. He didn't understand the feeling. Ty didn't get nervous around girls. Hadn't since....

He froze, his feet growing roots right there on the front lawn. He hadn't been nervous around girls since River Lee left, almost like he knew he didn't need to worry about ending up with any of them. Like all those relationships would never be serious, never be long-lasting, because those girls weren't River Lee.

As if the sky had clouded over and a storm had struck, fear bolted through Ty. He'd carried a soft spot for River Lee since their summer fling all those years ago, true. He liked her a lot, true. He wanted to get to know her better, true.

But also true was that if he did, he'd have to be patient. He'd have to be serious. And he'd have to stop dancing.

"She's worth it," he mumbled to himself as he got his feet going again. "And you're tired of dancing anyway."

And for the first time, Ty believed himself.

———

As River Lee and her mother cleaned up their backyard picnic, Ty lifted Hannah onto his shoulders and took Lexi by the hand. "We're gonna walk over to the duck pond," he told River Lee, a sliver of joy slicing through him. He hadn't realized how fulfilling a family could be. His sisters had left a long time ago, and meals with his parents just weren't the same as the lively, boisterous affair he'd just participated in.

Soda had been spilled, and mayo smeared everywhere, and River Lee had smiled and taken care of everything. She'd changed into cutoffs that showed the length of her legs and a tank top the color of ripe peaches. She'd told her girls stories about the time her and Ty were in high school, and he liked listening to her version of that summer.

"Give me a minute, and I'll come," she said.

"We won't walk fast." He took the girls around the side of the house to the front sidewalk, and sure enough, River Lee joined them before they'd even reached the end of the street.

"I brought some bread." She held up a zipper bag with two slices inside. "You girls are going to have to take a nap when we get back."

Neither of them complained, and Ty said, "Can I take a nap too?"

River Lee laced her hand through his free elbow and giggled. "I think you have yard work to do at your mom's."

"Oh, yeah, I do." He flashed her a smile and turned the corner. He hadn't grown up on this side of Gold Valley, but everyone knew about this duck pond. He'd ridden his bike to it with his family almost every Sunday morning before church. After church, they'd go to the monthly picnic or to the waterfalls, and the fact that Ty didn't have any of his own personal traditions suddenly registered.

He worked too much, he reasoned. When he had time off, he just wanted to ride his horse or relax with a bite to eat.

"I don't remember us sneaking into that movie," he said, repositioning his grip on Lexi's hand.

"You lifted the rope to the balcony and ushered me under," she said. "We barely made it around the corner before we heard someone talking in the lobby."

"We went up into the balcony?" The theater in town had never opened the balcony for a movie, not that Ty knew of.

He searched his memory for the time he'd gone up there with River Lee. He thought he remembered everything they'd done together.

"I sort of remember that now," he said as the memory, dark and blurry as it was, floated forward. "There were only a few rows of seats, and they weren't even bolted to the ground."

She laughed. "It was scary, actually. I thought we might fall through the floor."

"We didn't stay," he said, remembering now. "We didn't even sit down."

"I wasn't going to sit in those seats. They looked like someone had been sick on them." She walked so close to him, every cell in Ty's body became hyperaware of her presence. "We went and—"

"We got ice cream and went to the waterfalls."

She sighed, the happy, content type of sigh Ty liked. "I love the waterfalls."

"I liked going there with you," he said, tightening his arm against hers. He slipped his fingers into hers, holding hands much more intimate than just having her arm linked in his. "That was pretty much the perfect summer for me." An echo of old bitterness edged his throat, but he swallowed it away. "Did you like that summer, River Lee?"

Their eyes met, and she didn't have to answer verbally for him to know she'd enjoyed that summer with him.

"Why do you insist on calling me River Lee?" she asked, genuine curiosity in her tone.

He lifted one shoulder into a shrug. "It's who you are."

"Not anymore."

"Yes," he said. "You're not 'just River.' Not to me. That just…doesn't fit with what I know about you. I even tried saying it to myself in the mirror." He chuckled, somewhat in disbelief that he'd admitted his trial run on her name to her. "It's just not you."

"It is exactly me, Ty," she said, a twinge of anger in her voice now. "You don't know me very well at all. I'm not the same as I was thirteen years ago."

"Sure you are," he argued. "So you went off and got a degree and had a couple of cute little girls. You're still River Lee Whitely to me." He glanced at her, and her stiff shoulders and pressed lips didn't deter him from adding, "And I liked her." He squeezed her hand. "I liked her then, and I like her now. A lot."

She softened, but only slightly, and in the next few seconds, they arrived at the pond. She released his hand and gathered her girls around her so they could toss chunks of bread to the quacking mass of ducks.

Ty stood a few feet back, watching and waiting for River Lee to invite him to join them. She never did. She didn't even glance over her shoulder to see where he'd gone. Frustration filled him, and he wondered if maybe he'd gone too fast for her. Admitting he liked her and all.

But she'd touched him first. She'd invited him to lunch at her mom's place. She seemed to like him too, even if she didn't say it outright in words he could hear. He saw it in her eyes, felt it in her touch, knew it by how she acted.

Maybe just try calling her River, he thought as the bread ran out. But he wasn't sure he could actually make his mouth do such a thing.

CHAPTER 9

"*T*ime to go," River Lee said, and Ty turned toward her voice. He'd taken Lexi around the pond a bit so she could see the duck nests.

"C'mon," he said to the five-year-old. "Your mom says we have to go."

Lexi put her hand in Ty's and went with him back to the path that edged the road. "Mom, can we come here tomorrow too?"

"Maybe, sweetie." River Lee glanced at Ty and darted her gaze away again. She'd been generating that cool vibe again since their conversation about her name.

"Maybe Mister Ty can take me," Lexi said.

"Sure," Ty said. "We can go after church." He glanced at River Lee and realized he'd said the wrong thing. "I mean, if your mom says it's okay."

Lexi trained her baby blue eyes on River Lee. "Mom?"

"I said maybe."

Ty wasn't sure why she didn't want to commit. There wasn't a picnic after church tomorrow, and surely she didn't have plans. They walked toward the corner in silence, the girls running ahead to look at a butterfly.

"Sorry, River." His tongue felt thick in his mouth, the absence of "Lee" so pronounced it practically floated in the air between them anyway. He slipped his hand into hers. "I'll check with you before tellin' her I can do things."

"Thank you," she practically whispered, her voice hoarse.

"Is there a reason you can't come to the pond tomorrow after church?" he asked.

She called to Lexi to wait at the corner, but made no effort to speed her steps to reach her. When she didn't answer his question, he said, "River?"

She paused and looked at him. He gazed back steadily, unsure of which emotion dominated her expression. She looked almost sad, but when she smiled, he wasn't sure. "I don't like it when you call me River." She reached up and brushed her fingertips across the brim of his cowboy hat.

A shiver sailed down his spine, and a crazy amount of heat pooled in his stomach, and she'd only touched his hat. "What am I supposed to call you, then?" He dipped his head closer to hers, trying to get a whiff of her perfume, her shampoo, something.

She shifted her feet closer to his, and he was rewarded with the soft floral scent of her perfume. He took a deep breath, not even bothering to hide the fact that he was, and ran his free hand up her bare arm. "River?"

Now close enough to kiss her, Ty fought the urge. He

didn't want to do it in broad daylight, for anyone to see. Number two, her girls waited a quarter of a block away. The magic between them sizzled though, and Ty couldn't fight his attraction, his desire, his need for her much longer.

So he stepped back. Broke all contact between them. Cleared his throat. "I better get goin'. My mom's lawn isn't gonna mow itself." He stepped, his stride long but so unsure, toward the corner.

"Come on, girls." He swept them both into his arms and crossed the street, never looking back to see if River Lee was coming.

———

River let Ty carry her kids back to her mother's. She let him charm his way into their hearts—her mother's included. Hers too, if she were being honest. The way he drawled her name, the way his rough-and-tumble hand felt in hers, the way the scent of his cologne sent clouds straight into her head spoke of how far she'd let him in.

Still, she wasn't sure about his declaration that she was the same person she'd been thirteen years ago. River knew she wasn't, and she didn't like that he viewed her as that teenage girl. Was that really who he saw when he looked at her?

With every step back to the house, she told herself to get over it. The man liked her—had said it right out loud. It didn't matter what name he called her, as long as he called her.

She chuckled to herself. "Shoulda told him that," she said. She really could use some lessons in flirting, but Ty didn't seem to be holding her inept ability to talk to him, tell him important things, or flirt with him against her.

She waited, leaning against the passenger door of his truck, while he took Lexi and Hannah inside. He returned a couple of minutes later, a smile stuck to his face that rivaled the power of the sun.

"Thanks for coming to lunch," she said, giving him a grin that paled in comparison to his.

He swept her off her feet, causing her to giggle, and into a tight embrace, his face pressed into the hollow of her neck. "Anytime, sweetheart." He set her back on her feet and pulled back. "Can I call you that?"

She punched his chest lightly. "River Lee is fine."

He arched his eyebrows. "It is?"

"I kinda like it when you say it."

"Only me, though, right?" His hands slipped around her again, drew her against his chest again, sweeter and softer this time.

"If I'm the only one you're going to dinner and lunch with, then yes. Only you."

He dropped his hands and fell back like she'd caught on fire. "What does that mean?" He peered at her, those dreamy eyes glittering under his cowboy hat. "You think I'm going out with other girls?"

River shrugged, though the thought had crossed her mind. "Katie said—"

"Blazes," he said under his breath. "I am gonna stop talkin' to Katie Chamberlain." He started around the front of his truck. "As soon as I call her and tell her to stop talkin' to you."

Because she thought he'd leave, she jumped into his truck at the same time he opened the driver's door. "I have to go to my parents'," he said. "I don't think you want to come."

"Don't call Katie," she said, folding her arms.

"I won't if you won't." He glared at her, as much passion in him as she remembered. She wondered—not for the first time since they'd been reunited a week ago—what it would feel like to kiss him now. Now that he was older. Now that she was.

"She just said that you don't consider yourself dating someone until you kiss them." She tightened her arms, trying to keep all the pieces of herself from spilling out all over his truck. "And…." She hardened her resolve and gave his glare back to him. "I don't want to be your summer fling."

He flinched liked she'd punched him, falling back against the window behind him. "River Lee," he said, his voice filled with all kinds of hurt. "I—I wouldn't—" He twisted, started the truck, and planted both hands on the steering wheel. His fingers flexed and tightened, flexed and tightened. "I have to go."

"Ty."

"Can you please get out?"

"No." She slid across the seat, her bare legs sticking a bit to the seat cover. "No, I will not get out. Not until you finish what you were going to say."

"I've said it all."

"That's not true."

"Isn't it?" He faced her, a dozen emotions racing across his beautiful face. "I just told you I liked you a lot. I let you bottle up what *you* should be saying. I come whenever you call me. I go wherever you want to go. And you still think I'm playing with you?" He pointed at her and then him. "This isn't a game to me, River Lee."

She swallowed, the surprise at his outburst making her mind go blank.

"I'm not seeing anyone else." He exhaled and faced forward again, his hands going back to the steering wheel. Flex and tighten. Flex and tighten. "I don't even *want* to see someone else."

"All right." River didn't know what else to say.

"In fact, I broke off the beginning of a relationship with someone else."

"Who was it?"

"You don't know her." Flex and tighten. Flex and tighten. "She's…young." He cleared his throat, and it sounded like he was gargling rocks. "I have to go."

She moved across the seat and opened the passenger door. She climbed out, turned back and leaned into the truck, and said, "I'm sorry, Ty."

He didn't look at her. Didn't move at all. "I'll call you later."

She nodded and closed the door. He left a moment later, and for the second time that day, River's stomach squirmed as she watched him drive away from her.

CHAPTER 10

*R*iver buried her feelings in flour and sugar, stirring in white chocolate chips, milk chocolate chips, and semi-sweet chocolate chips. She knew her time with Ty was limited to weekends only. So why had she said "maybe" about going to pond tomorrow after church? The connection between them was as strong and hot as ever, as if she hadn't married someone else, lived with him for nine years, and borne two of his children.

Ty adored chocolate, if his inhalation of her mother's chocolate cake last weekend was any indication. And she couldn't face him without bringing a gift to apologize for her behavior. She didn't remember everything being so hot and cold with them previously, but now she either wanted him to hold her hand, breathe her in, and kiss her, or she needed him to take a giant step back. Slow down. Give her space and time to think.

She scooped cookies onto the sheet, the oven heated and

ready. "That's because you don't trust how you feel," she muttered to herself. And she didn't. John had taken a lot from her when she'd found out about his mistress, but the biggest one was her confidence to believe in herself. She thanked the Lord everyday that she'd already earned her degree so she didn't have to try to convince herself she was smart enough to help other people with their personal problems.

She'd been excited about the job at Silver Creek, because she knew it would never involve couples counseling. She wouldn't have to reveal how fraudulent she felt to fix relationships. After all, she hadn't been able to fix her own.

She slid the cookies into the oven and set the timer, thinking through the painful months in Las Vegas. Painful months she couldn't get back. Painful months she wouldn't want to repeat, but also painful months she was glad she'd endured.

She'd tried to fix her marriage with John. She'd been willing to forgive him, go to counseling with him, put everything behind them and start over. She'd been willing because of Lexi and Hannah, then only three and one.

But *he* hadn't been willing, and that had taken everything from her. She'd never felt so unwanted, and she'd tried to shield her girls from that. Thankfully, they were young enough not to understand much, and John worked long hours anyway, so his physical departure from the house was mostly an emotional crisis for River alone.

She'd requested full custody, citing John's complete unwillingness to attend counseling to repair the relationship, and had won. He hadn't even fought her on it, another testament to how unlovable and unnecessary to him she was.

Las Vegas became the place where River became obsolete, but she couldn't leave until everything was final. When it was, she packed up, sold the house, and headed north. She hadn't regretted it for a single day—until today. Until she made the usually-jovial and good-natured Ty Barker upset.

The timer went off, and River startled away from the kitchen counter where she'd been lost in thought. She checked the cookies, set them for one more minute, and picked up her phone.

She called Ty, sure he'd ignore her if she just texted. She wasn't much of a texter anyway. After everything with John, she'd learned it was always better to talk things out. She half-chuckled, half-sobbed as she realized she hadn't done with Ty what she'd learned to do. She hadn't spoken her mind, hadn't told him how she was feeling. Just like he'd said.

"River Lee?" His voice penetrated the fog in her mind, and it sounded like it wasn't the first time he'd said it.

"Yeah." She straightened. "Yes. Ty, hello." The reason for her call escaped her and she fumbled for her next words. Ty let her suffer in her silence, and she finally blurted, "I made cookies."

"That's great, sweetheart. Congratulations."

"I was wondering if you were still at your mom's." The timer went off and River pulled the cookies from the oven and set them on the stovetop. "Maybe you'd be more accepting of my apology if you were sweetened up a little."

"I'm perfectly sweet," he said, scoffing. "How many cookies have you eaten?"

"None, yet. They just came out of the oven."

"Eat a couple and then call me back." He hung up without telling her if he was still at his parents' house or not. She pulled the phone from her ear and stared at it, sure he had just covered the end of his phone and that was why the line had gone dead. But no, the call had ended.

Fury and frustration combined into a powerful tornado in her core. She dialed him back, one hand on her hip. He answered on the first ring. "Wow, did you stuff those two cookies in your mouth?"

"Did you just hang up on me?"

"No," Ty said. "I'm in a dead spot."

River huffed. "You're a big fat liar."

"I'm parked out front if you want to bring me some cookies." He chuckled, the sound coming through her phone still shiver-inducing. "And I'm going to hang up now."

"Fine," she said, ripping the phone away from her ear and hanging up before she had to listen to his side go silent again. She glanced at the still-sheeted cookies, seriously considering chucking them in the trashcan.

The scent of warm sugar and chocolate got the better of her, and she plucked a cookie from the tray and bit into it. Her eyes rolled back into her head, and Ty would have to have damaged taste buds not to enjoy this treat. After only one bite, he'd have to be more accepting of her apology. She slapped several cookies onto a paper plate, called down the hall that she was running outside for a second, and pulled open the front door. Shoeless, she ran across the front lawn to Ty's truck, which idled in its spot on the curb.

She slid the cookies across the seat toward him before climbing in. "I only ate one, just so you know."

"Hmm." He selected a cookie and held it toward her.

"I don't need to be sweetened up."

"Neither do I."

"You were angry with me."

"You implied I was dating a bunch of women, including you, at the same time."

"I know." She reached for the cookie and pinched it between two fingers. He didn't let go, and the moment between them locked. She couldn't look away from him even if she wanted to—and she didn't. "I'm sorry about that. I—" River swallowed at the same time Ty released the cookie.

She lifted it to her lips and took a bite. She chewed slowly, watching Ty's throat as he swallowed as if he were the one eating the treat. "I am a master baker." Her voice sounded breathy and weak, and she leaned toward Ty.

He slanted toward her too, and River's eyes drifted closed as she took another bite. "You should have one."

"I will." He took a cookie and leaned back, breaking the spell between them. River's muscles quivered and collapsed, everything inside her going soft.

She waited until he finished, until he said, "That was

delicious." His fingers scrabbled over hers until they aligned. "Thank you."

River squeezed his hand, the words she needed to say crowding her mouth. "Ty, I—I just need more time than normal girls do."

"More time for what?"

"More time to figure things out. How I feel. What I want to do after church tomorrow. That kind of stuff."

"I have time."

She turned her head toward him. "Do you?"

"For you, River Lee, I'd wait forever."

———

Ty couldn't believe he'd said such a romantic thing. He'd felt it though. Wanted to give River Lee the time she clearly needed. The alternative if he didn't wasn't acceptable to him.

A smile bloomed on her face, highlighting her best features: her eyes, her lips, and her neck.

"That's a nice thing to say," she said, her head lolling back to the center. He felt forever far away from her, though only a few feet separated them and he was holding her hand.

"I have a question for you," he said. "And you might want to take the week to think about how to answer it."

"The whole week?" Her tension skyrocketed, and Ty wished he didn't quite have the same senses as horses did to perceive how others felt.

"I mean, I won't see you until next Saturday."

"I'll see you after church tomorrow. We can take Lexi to the duck pond."

Hope soared through Ty, and he smiled, deciding on the spot to press his luck. "What about *at* church? Maybe you'd let me sit by you." He lifted their joined hands. "Do something like this."

She grinned, a lazy smile that made him want to fast-forward through time. "Is this allowed in church?"

"I think so, sure."

"Have you ever held a woman's hand in church?"

A bit of embarrassment leaked through him, making his neck heat up. "Yeah, sure. It's the best place. She can't run away."

River Lee burst out laughing, and Ty joined her, glad their previous awkwardness had gone. He'd never been so hurt as when she'd implied he was two-timing her. Ty was a lot of things, but a cheater he wasn't. And in fact, he wasn't even a lot of things. He kissed pretty women. Big deal. He didn't lead them on. He didn't sleep with them. He twirled them around the dance floor, and bought them ice cream and flowers, and took them on dates. Sometimes those dates ended with a kiss, and sometimes they didn't.

All the relationships had ended, as Ty had known they would.

But this thing with River Lee.... This thing with River Lee felt huge, all-encompassing, and absolutely terrifying. He felt like he was navigating unknown terrain, without food and water, without a map.

"Have you ever kissed a woman in church?"

"No, ma'am. The only people I see doin' that are gettin' married or already are. I've never done that."

"Ah, finally. One thing I've done that you haven't." The twinkle in her eye dimmed, and Ty leaned toward her and lifted her hand to his lips.

"I have an early morning, sweetheart. I'm afraid we'll have to leave it here."

"You didn't ask me the question."

"You want it right now? I can save it until tomorrow."

River Lee shook out her hair and straightened. "No, I can handle it."

He cocked his head and studied her. "All right. I was just wondering why you got divorced and moved back to Gold Valley."

She giggled, the sound much too high. It bounced around the cab, his brain, the sky. "You haven't heard?"

"No, ma'am. I don't spend a lot of time gossiping." He gave her a look he hoped would drive home his point. "I usually just go straight to the source when I need to know something."

Her face blanched and she tried to pull her fingers from his. He held on fast, and chuckled. "I get it, River Lee. I scare you."

She swallowed. "A little, I'm not gonna lie."

He leaned forward, thrilled beyond belief when she did too. "It's okay," he whispered. "You scare me too." He pulled back before the combined smell of chocolate and her perfume drove him to do something he couldn't take back. Couldn't apologize for.

He let go of her hand, and she reached for the door handle. "Church tomorrow then."

"Church tomorrow," he confirmed, watching as she slid gracefully from his truck, noticing the strip of skin on her back that showed when her shirt rode up a little. He licked his lips and looked away, too warm and too wanting. "See you later, sweetheart."

"Bye, Ty." Her voice carried a coy note, but Ty didn't have the guts to look at her again. Between all the talking, the hand-holding, the cookie-eating, no amount of air conditioning would be able to cool him down if he didn't leave right this moment. She needed time, and in order to give her that, he needed distance.

The passenger door closed, and Ty released the breath he'd been holding. He didn't make it down the block before a grin the size of Texas landed on his face and stayed there for the whole drive back to Horseshoe Home.

"What are you so happy about?" Caleb asked as Ty climbed out of his truck. His friend paused in his walk toward the cattle pens, where Ty knew Caleb did his bookkeeping on Saturday evenings.

He tossed Caleb the last cookie and said, "River Lee Whitely."

Caleb caught the treat and took a bite. "Ah, Ty's got himself a new girl."

Ty shook his head and gestured for Caleb to keep on toward his office. "She's no girl."

"But she is yours."

That slip of fear Ty had experienced expanded in his chest. "I'd like her to be." He put a hand on Caleb's arm, causing the other man to stop again and look at him. Really look. "For a lot longer than a couple of weeks too." Ty swallowed, his eyes searching Caleb's.

Caleb tipped his head back and laughed. "Oh, boy. I can see you're in trouble." He clapped him on the back. "Come help me get the schedule done for feeding this week."

Ty wanted to argue that planning the feeding of the cattle wasn't his job, but he went with Caleb anyway. For some reason, he didn't want to be alone with his thoughts tonight.

"Wait. You're not going to the dance?" Caleb slanted his eyebrows at Ty. "That's unlike you. You're not helping tonight?"

"The dance!" Ty froze. "I totally forgot." He spun and hurried toward his truck, pulling his phone from his pocket as he went so he could call Kevin, the director of the summer dances.

Caleb's pounding laugh sounded behind him. "This girl must really have you in knots!" he called, adding another laugh to punctuate the statement.

CHAPTER 11

$\mathcal{T}$y's knots tangled as he drove down the canyon. Though he was late, and he hated being late, he took his time on the road. The drive from Gold Valley to Horseshoe Home in the summer was beautiful. The green trees, the evergreens, the white bark, the mountain rivers, all of it calmed Ty's ragged soul.

As he rounded the corner and came down to the water-falls, he turned off and parked. He rolled the window down and listened to the roar of the falls as the water poured over them. Shaped like a horseshoe—and after which the ranch was named—the falls always enveloped Ty in a sense of peace.

He'd spent some time with River Lee hiking around the falls, but he'd never kissed her here. He added that item to his summer to-do list, hoping kissing was near the top of her list too. With her confession that she needed lots of time to pretty much do anything, Ty gazed at the water and let the laughter of the children and families convince him that he could go slow.

If only slow was his style. "It can be," he told himself. "You just drove down the mountain pretty slow." Ty knew it was different for him with women, but he was dedicated to doing as much as possible to keep River Lee as close as possible.

The idea that he should call River Lee and invite her to the dance popped into his mind. He tried to push it away, but it kept circling around and around until he picked up his phone and put in a call.

"Miss me already?" she answered, her voice upbeat. It made his pulse pound to hear her so happy.

"Always," he said, playing the game. "I'm actually on my way to the dance, and I wondered if maybe you had the time and energy to stop by?" He pressed his eyes closed and waited, his breath stuck somewhere in his throat.

"How late does the dance usually go?"

"About eleven."

"That's pretty late."

"We don't have to stay the whole time. And there will be refreshments." He singsonged the last word, hoping to attract her to the park with the promise of sweets.

"The girls do go to bed at eight-thirty...."

"So maybe you could come after that," he pressed.

"I'll talk to my mother."

Ty hesitated. "You think she'll have plans?"

"She hasn't said anything, but there's this guy she's mentioned a time or two...I just need to talk to her first."

"Okay, well, if I see you, I see you." He bit back the next words he wanted to say: *I hope I see you.* She knew that already; no need to put the additional pressure on her.

He pulled onto the road and continued to the square. He had to leave his truck farther away than normal because he was so late, but he ate up the distance soon enough. "I'm so sorry," he said to Kevin once he arrived. The refreshment tables had already been set up, and the crew only had two more rows to place before the dance floor was complete. "Should I do the punch?"

"Yeah, start there." Kevin sent Ty with a woman named Jillian to get the refreshments, the cooler for punch, and the drink mix. He carried a huge box of cookies while she grabbed the cooler, and together, they had the refreshments out just as the first dancers arrived.

Ty snagged a cookie and ate it, having skipped dinner in order to patch things up with River Lee. This chocolate chip concoction was seriously lacking, especially compared to River Lee's treats. Though twilight hadn't quite settled yet, more and more people kept coming, and Ty got busy replacing napkins and wandering around picking up empty cups.

During that chore, he used to scope out the girls who had come and find one he wanted to ask to dance once night truly fell. Now, he focused on his work, his silent phone in his pocket driving him mad.

Dusk came, but River Lee did not. Ty resisted the urge to check the time. He knew what time the sun went down in mid-June, and her girls had gone to bed an hour ago. He pushed away his negative thoughts and feelings and collected another pile of garbage.

"Hey, Ty."

His heart pumped out an extra beat as he glanced up. But Whitney stood a few feet away, wearing a tight, black dress that barely covered the necessary parts. She bit her lip and shuffled her feet.

"Hey, Whitney." He settled his weight away from her and glanced around for her usual posse of friends. He couldn't see them. "How've you been?"

She rushed him and put both palms flat against his chest. "Lonely without you."

"All right." He stepped back to get her hands off him, hoping she wouldn't topple forward or grab onto him again. "I see Troy over there. He's lookin' lonely too." He nodded toward the other side of the dance floor, glad when Whitney gave him a pout before mincing away.

He blew out his breath and turned around, coming toe-to-toe with River Lee. She tucked a curled lock of hair behind her ear and looked over his shoulder.

"She one of your old girlfriends?"

Ty checked over his shoulder too. "She's the one I broke up with last weekend."

"Oh." River blushed, and under the gentle lighting hanging from the trees, Ty didn't think he'd ever seen anything so beautiful. His fingers twitched toward her, but he fisted them and nodded toward the dance floor.

"Do you dance?"

"Badly." She giggled, and glanced at her feet. "And honestly, I can barely walk in these shoes."

Ty let his eyes slide down the length of her body, enjoying the silky, bright green blouse against her tan skin, as well as the black shorts she'd paired with it. A pair of strappy, tall heels adorned her feet, and Ty let himself reach for her arm. "Yeah, those look dangerous." His voice broke on the last word, and adrenaline rushed through him when his skin met hers.

She slid her hand up his arm and into his. "I believe you tried to lure me here with refreshments."

He snorted. "I did not *lure* you here. I *enticed.*" He steered her onto the hard floor so her heels wouldn't sink into the grass.

"That you did." She smiled at him, and it lit up his whole world. His chest warmed and he returned the gesture, gripping her hand tighter when her step wobbled.

He noticed several other men eyeing them, and he knew they weren't looking at him. Ty didn't want to share River Lee with anyone, and after he handed her a plastic cup of punch, he said, "Maybe we should skip the dancing tonight."

Her bright eyes filled with alarm. "I don't think I can skip in these heels." She sipped her punch as LeRoy Jones approached the table.

"Hey, River." He swept his cowboy hat off his head, and Ty suppressed a growl. "Do you wanna dance?"

Pure panic paraded across River Lee's face, and she choked on her punch. Her gaze landed on Ty, and it was clear she wanted—no, *needed*—his help. He stepped back and let her handle it, curious to see how she'd save herself when she showed up wearing heels that high and shorts that short.

He cleared his throat, realizing *why* she'd worn those things, and ducked his head.

"I'm—I'm sorry," River Lee said, her voice set on sugar-sweet. She indicated Ty. "I'm here with him."

LeRoy glanced at Ty, nodded, and faded back onto the dance floor, his face reddening under the dim light.

River spun to him. "Let's get out of here."

Ty chuckled. "Now you're talkin'. But you can't blame the guy. You look great tonight." He tucked her against his side and went to check out with Kevin. That done, they escaped the party atmosphere of the dance in favor of somewhere quieter.

River Lee only made it half a block before she bent to remove the shoes. She sank to her regular height and sighed. "Learn something new everyday."

"Oh yeah?" Ty didn't let her get too far from him. "What did you learn today?"

She nudged him with her shoulder. "Several things. Number one, you can be bribed with cookies."

He laughed, sobering quickly. "I think any man can be bribed with homebaked goods, sweetheart."

"Number two, you look great under Christmas lights."

"I didn't even change my clothes," he said.

"Number three, I shouldn't wear heels if I have further than five feet to walk."

"Or if you don't want men to ask you to dance."

She giggled and draped herself over his arm. "That was so embarrassing. I didn't know what to say."

"You handled it just fine."

"No thanks to you."

"I didn't tell you to wear that blouse." He fingered the silky fabric, a rush of desire nearly knocking him senseless. "Or those shorts, and definitely not those shoes."

"Men are so predictable."

"Is that the fourth thing you learned today?"

"No, I've known that for years." She giggled, and the warm, soft sound washed over him.

Ty hummed, the town around them peaceful in the dark. He liked that he didn't have to talk to be comfortable with River Lee. He took a deep breath of her hair, enjoying the silence with her.

"I divorced my husband, John, because he was cheating on me with his secretary."

Ty stumbled, completely not expecting River Lee to say that. He immediately disliked the man and squeezed her hand. "I'm so sorry."

"It was hard at first. It's been a while since I found out. A year since the divorce went through."

"Do you think about it—about what he did—a lot?"

"Not often, no." She took a deep breath and exhaled heavily. Ty wanted to erase her past pain, provide a soft place for her to land.

"I came to Gold Valley because I'd been gone a long time, and my mother wanted me to. Plus, there was a good job here, and I needed it. And." Her voice went up in pitch. "And I'd lost myself in Las Vegas."

Ty nodded and let a few seconds of silence settle into the night. "Have you found her here?"

She tipped her head back and smiled at him. "Sort of. She's a work-in-progress."

Ty spotted a bench in front of the closed bakery and eased onto it, exhaustion enveloping him as he sat. He groaned. "It's been a long day. Sit with me?"

She complied, positioning herself right next to him, and he lifted his arm and draped it over her shoulders. "I don't like Saturdays," she said, snuggling closer.

"No? You've disliked our day together?"

"I dislike horseback riding." She rolled her head from side to side, finally letting it come to rest against his chest.

"You'll get used to it."

"It feels like my bones are grinding against each other." She stretched her shoulders.

He dipped his head closer to hers. "I've rather enjoyed today." Despite its ups and downs, ending the day with River Lee in his arms practically erased the couple of hours he'd stomped around his mother's yard, trying to get blades of grass all the same height.

She tipped her face back and he leaned down. Only a few inches separated them, and with anyone else Ty wouldn't have hesitated, wouldn't have given kissing her an extra thought. But with River Lee, he did both.

"How long are you going to make me wait?" she whispered. "My neck's starting to get a crick."

"You want me to kiss you?"

Her eyes drifted closed and open again as a playful smile crossed her face. "Very badly."

Ty didn't wait another moment, didn't give kissing River Lee any more hesitation. He closed the distance between them and touched his lips to hers, seeking, probing for the right match between them.

He breathed in, a sliver of space between them before kissing her again, this time their mouths meeting in perfect tandem. She twisted to face him, her fingers tracing up his throat and the side of his face to land in the hair on the back of his neck. He shivered despite the warm night, this second kiss with River Lee even more spectacular than the first.

The fireworks between them popped and sparked and Ty never wanted to kiss another woman again.

———

The hair on the back of Ty's neck was soft and wonderful. The strength in his arms as he held her close, the tenderness of his touch as he cupped her face and kissed her more completely than she thought she could be kissed.

She'd thought their first kiss had changed her life, but with his lips on hers again, she realized now that she'd been wrong back then. She couldn't believe she'd left for college after he'd kissed her.

As he pulled away and chuckled, River Lee kept her eyes closed, drinking in this moment and committing it to memory. She sent a prayer of gratitude heavenward. Gratitude that she'd been led back to Gold Valley, even if the path here hadn't been easy and she wouldn't wish it on anyone.

She laughed softly with him as her hand slid down to his chest. "I promise I won't leave in three weeks this time."

"That would be great," Ty whispered. His chest lifted as he took a deep breath. "I didn't mean to kiss you so fast, River Lee."

"Maybe you better do it again," he said. "And go slower so we can both enjoy it."

"You didn't enjoy that, sweetheart? I can definitely try again." And he did, and River Lee lost track of everything but the taste of him, the smell of him, the very solid presence of him next to her.

CHAPTER 12

*R*iver sighed, her heartbeat still erratic, as she leaned against the closed front door. She imagined Ty just on the other side of it, where he'd just given her the best goodnight kiss of her life.

The best night of her life, period.

Giddiness galloped through her the way wild horses did out on the prairie. She hummed to herself and went into the kitchen to fix a glass of iced sweet tea. Heat had draped itself over everything, and River wondered if she'd ever be cool again.

She'd just get the smell of Ty out of her nose when she'd feel a phantom of his hands on her waist, causing her skin to dance in delight and a smile to slide across her face. Gulping the sweet tea to reduce her core temperature, River stepped down the hall to check on Lexi and Hannah.

She choked on her tea. Her girls. She'd forgotten about them completely while she'd been out with Ty. Guilt streamed through her as if someone had opened the flood-gates on a dam. She gripped the doorframe for support and ducked into their bedroom. They slept, completely unaware of her erratic emotions.

Lexi snored softly, her stuffed elephant clutched against her chest while Hannah had kicked all the covers off and curled into a ball to sleep. River set the sweet tea on the dresser and wandered to the edge of the double bed the girls shared. She traced her fingers along Hannah's hairline, a war beginning inside.

They'd already been through so much. Their father leaving, a move across several state lines, a mother who now worked five days a week and had to subject herself to horseback riding on the sixth. Could she really start dating Ty?

She reasoned that Lexi and Hannah had taken to Ty just fine, that they were young and resilient. Still, her chest felt like an expanded balloon, one breath away from exploding. She collected her sweet tea from the dresser and escaped to her own bedroom.

Her thoughts played seesaw, first on a high from kissing Ty, then sinking to the low worries about her girls. She finally fell asleep some time after midnight, riding the adrenaline of that delicious kiss.

She woke because of a dream where John showed up in the dead of winter and demanded she let him see Lexi and Hannah. She hadn't seen what choice she had—he did have visitation rights, just not custody. He'd taken the girls out to lunch, but he'd never returned.

Never brought the girls back at all.

River's heart tried to pound a hole through her breastbone, and she pressed one hand over her pulse to calm it. Sun shone through the window. River fumbled for her phone to check the time.

She saw the nine in the first digit and kicked the blankets from her legs. She'd be late to church if she didn't get showered right now. Lexi's voice filtered down the hall as River strode in that direction. Her mother—her wonderful, caring mother—stood at the dining room table with her granddaughters.

"You made breakfast?" River asked.

"Muffins on Sunday," her mom said. "Always."

"We didn't have muffins last Sunday."

"But Miss Lexi asked for muffins on Sundays." She beamed at the little girl. "So she gets muffins on Sundays."

One of River's hands floated to her throat. "I used to make them muffins every Sunday." Her voice barely made it out of her throat. The fact that Lexi could remember that suggested that maybe they had more memories of Las Vegas and their father than River gave them credit for. A viper struck inside her chest, causing a pinch of pain to radiate outward to all her limbs.

"Coffee in the kitchen." Her mom nodded behind River.

But River shook her head. Caffeine would only make her jumpier. "I need to go shower. As soon as I'm out, you girls will need to get in the tub. Church today." She turned away as Lexi asked if she had to wash her hair.

"Yes, baby. You have to wash your hair. I'll help you, okay?" River placed a kiss on her daughter's forehead and hurried to get ready. She dressed while the tub filled for the girls, and she hitched up her skirt to kneel and wash two little towheads so they could all get to church on time.

River skipped eating entirely, her stomach sour and swimming with sharks. She left the heels in the back of her closet and opted for a more sensible pair of two-inch wedges to go with her knee-length pink sundress. The summer breeze toyed with the skirt as she lifted Hannah to her hip and gripped Lexi's hand in hers.

The walk to the chapel felt somewhat like a death march, with too many pairs of eyes glancing her way. She wondered if they'd all been talking about her and Ty sneaking away from the dance. Main Street had been pretty deserted, and she didn't think anyone had seen them kissing on the bench in front of the bakery.

Still, she felt like everyone knew, like she wore the information like headlines on her face. She herded the girls onto a bench, barely sitting when Ty bent down and said, "Mornin'."

Everything darkened for a second, like the power had blinked out. Her heart stopped completely, but somehow she managed to smile up at him. "Hey."

"Do you guys have room for one more?"

"Sure." River twisted back to the girls. "Scooch over, Lexi. Mister Ty is gonna sit with us."

Hannah climbed over River's legs and lifted her arms up for Ty to pick her up. River's heartbeat exploded back into motion as he swept the little girl off her feet with a smile as genuine and gentle and giant as the state of Texas.

He took up the space at the end of the bench and balanced Hannah on his left knee as he swept his right arm around River and pulled her into his side.

"This isn't holding hands," she hissed.

"Oh, I'm sorry." His tone mocked her, and she swatted his leg with a muffled giggle.

His lips touched her forehead like a whisper just as the pastor got up. "Good morning," he said. "Summer is my favorite time of the year." He beamed over the congregation. "I'd like to talk to you today about keeping the Lord at the forefront of all you do and say. Are you His example? When people interact with you, do they see something different?"

River cocked her head, trying to follow Dr. Pinnion's line of reasoning. He had a soothing voice, and combined with Ty's heady scent and River's late night, she found her attention wandering.

Before she knew it, the service had ended, but Ty didn't move. She glanced at him, her brain sort of sloshing around in her skull.

"She's asleep," he whispered, glancing down at a slumbering Hannah in his arms. "I don't know what to do."

River's heart swelled with love, and she tried to make it stop. Go away. Something. She'd been reunited with Ty for eight days. Eight days. She couldn't be falling in love with him already.

"I'll take her." She reached for Hannah, waking the girl as she gathered her from Ty. "Lexi, get all your crayons now."

"Mom, are we goin' to the duck pond?" Lexi didn't

gather her crayons. She stood at River's elbow, a hopeful look on her face.

"Yes, baby. Now get cleaned up."

"After lunch," Ty said. "Right, Miss Whitely?"

River found him looking at her mother, and she sensed Ty had been communicating behind her back. She swung her gaze back to Ty, who grinned like the devil himself. "What's going on?" she asked.

"I'm starving," he said.

The chapel was nearly empty, and River exhaled. "Mom didn't make anything for lunch." Now that River thought about it, the fact that her mom hadn't made lunch was strange. Her throat itched like she'd swallowed frantic butterflies. "Ty."

"We're goin' to lunch with my folks."

River's eyebrows shot toward her hairline. "All of us?"

"All y'all." He backed into the aisle. "My mother makes a mean potato salad, I'll have you know."

River followed him, practically wielding Hannah like a shield between her and Ty. "I've had your mother's potato salad. She wins every year at the Harvest picnic."

"And it's good, right?"

"It's great." River turned back to the pew. "Come on, baby." Lexi stepped into the aisle, latching her hand onto Ty's whether he liked it or not. River had met his parents several times. She wasn't sure why she felt like throwing up, other than she would've liked some time to prepare for lunch with his parents.

It always came down to having more time. A sense of

self-loathing flickered through River. She didn't want to miss out on something great because she wanted to analyze everything to death.

She exited the chapel, and Ty slipped his free hand into hers. "Are you upset about the lunch?"

She shook her head, her voice caught behind her tongue, behind her emotions. She wasn't upset with him. She was upset with herself. She needed to figure out how to get out of her own way, because a guy like Ty wouldn't hang around forever.

———

Ty could see something awry in River Lee. Heck, a blind man would've been able to tell simply because of the amped up vibes she emitted into the atmosphere. He couldn't shake Lexi's hand out of his, though, so he just kept walking. He helped Lexi into the sedan while River Lee buckled Hannah into a car seat.

"We're headed over right now?" River Lee wouldn't look at him, and she hugged herself as if cold, though the summer sun torched everything it touched.

"You can go change if you want." He stepped closer to her and trailed his fingers up her bare arm, a shiver infecting him as it shook her shoulders. "You don't have to come. I just thought it would be nice. A bit of a change."

The smile she sent in his direction seemed a bit stretched around the edges. "I like anything I don't have to make myself."

He leaned down and pressed his lips to her forehead. "All right. Let's go then." Ty tucked his hand in hers and tugged her toward his truck.

River Lee looked over her shoulder at the sedan as her mother slid behind the wheel. "She's—we're—?"

"She'll meet us there." Ty kept his feet moving toward his pickup. "Do you want me to stop by your place so you can change?"

River Lee shook her head, her steps landing a bit closer to him. She laid her cheek against his bicep, and a surge of satisfaction roared through Ty with the force of a tidal wave. He squeezed her fingers, unsure of how to articulate anything in that moment.

The drive happened with low country music in the background and River Lee sitting right next to him on the bench seat. She hummed along with the songs, her attitude completely different now.

He pulled up to the curb in front of his parents' house and flipped the truck into park. He half-turned toward River Lee at the same time she faced him. "You ready?"

She stretched up and kissed him, her lips soft and sweet against his. She broke the connection long before he was ready to let her go. "Now I'm ready."

He twisted away from her and got out of the truck before he kissed her again. He rapped on the front door at the same time he opened it, his right hand tightly secured in River Lee's. "Ma? Dad?"

"There you are." His mom poked her head around the wall leading into the kitchen. "Come in, come in." She wiped her sudsy hands on her apron as she entered the living room with a smile. "River Lee, look at you."

Ty watched River Lee for a reaction. She tolerated him calling her River Lee, but he wasn't sure how she'd react to his mother doing it. She beamed at the older woman, released Ty's hand, and accepted the hug his mother offered.

"Good to see you again, Charlotte," River Lee said. "What do you need help with?"

His mom waved her hand like she'd had the entire meal catered. "Nothing. Come on back. We're going to eat on the deck." She glanced over River Lee's shoulder. "Where are your girls?"

"My mother was right behind us." River Lee slipped her fingers back into Ty's as she followed his mom around the corner and into the kitchen. Ty's spirits rose with how easily she moved in the house, how charismatic she was, how charitable.

She caught him grinning and lifted her eyebrows in a silent question. He shook his head. "Where's Dad?"

"He's building a fire. He thought the girls would like to make s'mores." His mom lifted a massive red bowl and handed it to Ty. "Take that out to the table, would you?"

Ty didn't really have a choice. He accepted the bowl of potato salad from his mom, balanced it against his chest with one arm so he could pick out a piece of potato with a chunk of carrot on it. He popped it into his mouth as his mother frowned.

"Ty."

"I can't help myself," he said, moving around the dining room table toward the backdoor. "Your potato salad is so good." He plucked up another bite, this time with a green pea in tow. He loved the creaminess from the sour cream and mayo. Loved the fresh vegetables—corn, peas, carrots, and green beans—among the potatoes. And his mother was a master at salting vegetables until they tasted good.

"Tell me your girls' names," his mom said as Ty stepped outside, and he increased his pace so he wouldn't have to leave River Lee alone for long.

"Hey, Dad." Ty set the bowl in its obvious place on the table and turned toward the fire pit, which sat several paces away from the shaded deck. Three towering pine trees kept the fire pit out of the sun as well, and kept the playground his father had installed when Vienna had her first child shady too.

"Ty." He poked at the almost charred logs in the pit. "River Lee here?"

"Mom is giving her the fifth degree."

His father chuckled. "I'm sure she is."

Ty wasn't sure what else to say. He saw his parents every Saturday, and he didn't have a lot going on in his life that he needed to talk about. When he'd proposed the idea of hosting River Lee, her girls, and her mother for lunch, his parents had been struck speechless for several seconds. Then his mother had flown into high gear by menu-making and giving Ty a list of things to clean before he left.

"So you like this woman," he dad said. It wasn't really a question.

"I always have," Ty said, his voice on the lower edge of audible.

"She's got two daughters."

"I'm aware." Ty didn't let any annoyance infuse his voice. His dad wasn't one to lecture, and Ty had learned over the past three decades of his life to appreciate the few things his dad did say.

"They gonna live with you on the ranch?"

Ty tipped his head back and laughed. The sound sailed into the sky, releasing the pent-up tension in Ty's shoulders. "Dad. She's been back in town for two weeks. We've spent a couple of days together."

His father met Ty's eyes, but he wasn't laughing. "Yeah, but you'd know by now if you didn't want to be with her."

"Dad—"

"And she has two girls. She wouldn't put them through something she didn't think she could see through to the end."

Ty shook his head, frustration foaming in the back of his mind. "Dad, please don't do this today. It's just lunch."

"All right." His dad lifted one hand in agreement.

Ty said, "Thank you," and started back toward the house, hoping River Lee wasn't being subjected to a similar conversation from his mother.

CHAPTER 13

*T*y leaned away from the picnic table, the blueness of the sky above him almost unbelievable. "Best lunch ever, Ma." He shot her one of his *I'm-your-favorite-son* grins, which always won her over. He'd learned the skill when he was only fifteen, and even when he got himself into a stitch or two of trouble, he could flash that grin and she'd soften considerably.

He couldn't remember the last time he'd brought a woman to meet his parents. As he watched Lexi and Hannah play on the swing set, he realized he'd *never* brought someone to meet his parents. He simply had never been serious about someone the way he was about River Lee.

His throat narrowed and his stomach felt overly full of brisket, bread, and that delicious potato salad. Still, he managed to sling his arm around River Lee's shoulders and enjoy the summer breeze coming through the trees. Her mother had eased some of the pressure on him to keep the conversation on the right topics, but he was ready to be alone with River Lee now.

"Should we go to the pond?" he asked.

Before River Lee could respond, a shrill wail filled the summer sky. His gaze anchored on the girls, one of whom was running toward them and one who was lying in the grass crying.

River Lee got up and hurried toward her daughters, scooping up Hannah and asking her what had happened. Ty had seen River Lee console her kids before, get them settled down, fix everything. She was remarkably good at it while Ty didn't have the first clue about what to do.

"Let me go see if she needs help." Her mom got up and crossed the deck, leaving Ty alone with his parents.

"She's a nice woman." His mom patted his hand as she stood. She gathered whatever leftovers she could carry and headed into the house.

The weight of his father's gaze stayed on Ty's face, and he finally looked at his dad. "Go on, then," he said.

His dad looked toward the playground and back to Ty. "You think you're ready to be a father?"

"Dad." Ty exhaled, the sound full of exasperation. "We've spent a couple of days together. We're not getting married tomorrow."

"You're not gettin' any younger." He hooked his thumb over his shoulder. "And neither is she."

Ty pushed himself up, his muscles as tired as this conversation. "All right, Dad."

"What will you do to support yourself and maybe a family when you can't ranch anymore?"

Ty paused, confusion racing through him at the topic change. "Why wouldn't I be able to ranch?"

His dad stood and stacked the plates. "All cowboys eventually become something else," he said. "That's all I'm sayin'." He lifted the dishes and left Ty to his thoughts.

And Ty didn't like where his thoughts went. He'd never given much thought to what he'd do when he got older, when his body wasn't as strong as it was now. Heck, he rarely thought much beyond that day's chores and activities.

As Lexi continued to cry, a sense of inadequacy dove through Ty, saturating his muscles, his bones, his very soul.

What do I do now? he thought, sending the thought toward heaven, hoping the Lord would tell him.

River Lee turned, frustration etched in the lines around her eyes. She marched back to him, Hannah balanced on one hip. "I need to take the girls home," she said. "They need naps."

"Oh, yeah, sure." Ty's heart plummeted to the tips of his boots, but he tried to infuse understanding and kindness into his voice. "We can go to the pond anytime."

As River Lee's mother brought a still sniffling Lexi closer, Ty crouched to be on the girl's level. "We'll go feed the ducks another time, 'kay?"

A fresh set of tears slid down her face. "We can't feed the ducks?" She switched her gaze to River Lee.

"No." A flush worked its way through River Lee's face, and her jaw clenched. "You need a nap." She turned and reached for her plate.

Ty leapt to intercept her. "You don't need to clean up."

She looked near tears herself. "I'm sorry," she murmured.

"Nothin' to be sorry about." He nudged her toward the backdoor. "I'll walk you out." Ty stuck a smile to his face and guided River Lee through the house, a mixture of emotions swirling through him until he couldn't separate them.

He stood back, out of place, as the girls got loaded into the car. River Lee brushed her fingertips along his before she turned and slid onto the passenger seat. Ty lifted his hand as they drove away, but nothing about the afternoon made him cheerful. Especially that he didn't even get to kiss River Lee goodbye.

———

River slept poorly that week. She suffered through bone-jarring horseback riding lessons that weekend and snuck off behind the cabin next to the barn to kiss Ty until she felt seconds away from passing out.

He went on over to his mother's and she took a much-needed nap. She saved him a seat on the pew next to her, and they held hands during the sermon. He didn't set up any more lunches with his family, and she didn't invite him over to her mother's to eat either.

Weeks passed after the same manner, and River knew

something was holding Ty back. He was affectionate, and sometimes he looked at her with such heat and desire in his eyes she thought she'd melt.

If his gaze wouldn't do it, the July sun in Montana would. As she dumped ice over the water bottles she'd put in the cooler, she called down the hall to her mother, "Did you get the sunscreen?"

The Fourth of July parade started at ten and usually lasted a good two hours. By noon, River would be ready to escape the sunshine even with sunscreen.

Her mom appeared at the mouth of the hall, a large bag slung over her shoulder. "Got it. And the licorice, and the dill pickle chips."

River smiled. "And I've got the water. Let's get the girls." She stepped to the sliding glass door and called for Lexi and Hannah to bring Pippa so they could go to the parade. All three of them came barreling toward the house, and River's mom scooped up the little dog and set her in the top of her bag.

"Ty said there was a spot saved across from McCall's," River said as her mom backed out of the driveway.

"I invited Milt to sit with us too," her mom said, and every red flag in River's mind rose.

"Milt?"

Her mom wouldn't look at her, and her voice sounded the tiniest bit squeaky when she said, "We're friends."

River wasn't sure how she felt. She didn't know her dad, and her mom had never seemed unhappy without him in her life. River knew she'd dated in the past, but for some reason, having a name and a face to go with the situation felt more personal.

"That's great, Mom."

Her mom laughed. "We're not engaged or anything. It's not a big deal." She finally cut a look in River's direction. "Not like you and Ty."

Warmth filled River at the mere mention of his name, as it had been doing for weeks. "I like him," she said carefully as if she were in one of her therapy sessions with Dr. Thatcher, the psychiatrist she'd been seeing since she got to town.

"And he certainly likes you." Her mom turned and they hit bumper-to-bumper traffic.

"We're not engaged either," River said. "It's not a big deal." The words felt false on her tongue—her relationship with Ty was a big deal to her. He seemed just as serious as she did, and all her previous fears about him had vanished.

Still, something wasn't quite right with him and she needed to find out what it was.

Today, she told herself as her mom admitted defeat and pulled to the side of the road. "We'll have to walk from here, girls," she said as she cut the engine and opened her door. "Everyone carries something."

River made sure she had a chair and the blessed cooler full of water before she allowed her mind to wander to Ty again. She'd obsessed over what could be bothering him and had come up blank every time.

Now, as the spot that had been roped off for the ranch came into view, just as much hopelessness crowded her lungs. At least a dozen cowboys loitered in the area, and River hesitated as she searched for the one face she wanted to see.

The crowd parted, and there Ty stood. He wore a casual pair of khaki shorts and a blue polo, a look she didn't see too often on the cowboy. His normal chocolate-brown cowboy hat sat in place, completing the picture of perfection. "Hey." He grinned at her with the wattage of the Vegas Strip, and she basked in the warmth of it.

"Hey, yourself." She stepped over the rope and handed him her camp chair. "I brought water."

"We load up on soda," he said as he lifted a mug the size of her head. Every cowboy seemed to have one, and River wondered if the foreman had them on soda rations. He set up her chair and her mom spread the blanket for the girls in front of that. River sat, and Ty pulled up a chair next to her. Her mom disappeared to the corner of the area with Milton, her not-so-secret boyfriend, but she left the bag with all the treats.

"This is a nice spot," River said as she scanned the street in front of them. "Shady."

Ty claimed her hand and lifted it to his lips. He kissed the inside of her wrist, making her feel alive in a way she hadn't before. "It's good to see you."

She flashed him a smile that felt like peanuts compared to his. This was the Ty she knew, the Ty who knew how he felt and wasn't afraid to show it. The Ty who looked at her like she was made of pure chocolate and he wanted to eat all of her. Right now.

"What's with you?" she asked with a teasing note in her voice.

"Horseshoe Home Ranch is up for sale," he said with a cat-ate-the-canary grin. "I'm gonna buy it."

CHAPTER 14

River blinked at Ty, her mind a jumbled mess. Such a jumbled mess, her brain couldn't send anything to her vocal chords.

Police sirens wailed in the distance, probably down by the elementary school where the parade began. River focused on the sound for several seconds, her thoughts finally organizing themselves.

"You're going to buy the ranch?" River's fingers tightened around Ty's. "I didn't realize…. Well, I don't know what I didn't realize."

A darkness River didn't understand and rarely saw danced across Ty's features. "I can't be a cowboy forever," he grumbled.

She leaned closer, sensing this conversation probably shouldn't be had in front of every cowboy currently employed at the ranch. "If you buy the ranch, you most certainly can."

His jaw clenched; his eyes blazed; his shoulders stiffened. "Exactly."

Before she could comprehend what that single word meant, Hannah squealed, stealing River's attention to the street. The street, which Hannah was now running toward as fast as her three-year-old legs would carry her.

"Hannah!" River bolted from her chair, all thoughts of Ty buying a century-old ranch forgotten. Her daughter nearly fell flat on her face as she stepped off the curb in her haste to get to the candy the high school mascot—a life-sized tiger—had thrown in their direction.

Hannah's chubby fist had just closed around a piece of saltwater taffy—seriously not worth the effort of even getting up—when River reached her. Children's bodies jostled her as they pounced on the candy like ravenous lions on fresh meat.

River scooped Hannah away from the fray, her heart bobbing in the back of her throat. "You don't just run into the street," River said in a stern voice. "You scared Mommy."

"Candy." Hannah squirmed and pointed, but the sweets had all been claimed.

"We have candy in the bag." River turned back to the grass to find Ty standing on the curb, concern in his delicious eyes. She bypassed him to set Hannah back on the blanket. "Look. Licorice." She pulled the bag out of her mother's purse and tossed it onto the ground near her kids, too tired to even open it for them. Lexi could do it, and she did, claiming three pieces of licorice before sharing with Hannah.

River collapsed back in her chair. Ty returned much slower, his throat moving as he swallowed hard. Again and then again.

"What?" she asked.

"Nothin'." He took her hand in his and focused his attention down the street, where the first police motorcycle had just rounded the corner.

River sensed the fib in Ty's single-word answer, but the deafening roar of the motorcycle engine prevented her from pushing him to tell her what was really going on. She churned through the idea of him owning Horseshoe Home Ranch. Living in the homestead all by himself—or maybe with her.

It took thirty minutes to drive from the waterfalls— which were already on the outskirts of town—to the ranch. Could she make that drive everyday to go to work, to take the girls to school, to buy groceries?

She shook her head and stood as the Boy Scouts who carried the flag approached. She shouldn't be worrying about a life she didn't have. She'd been back in town for six weeks and had been reunited with Ty for five. They weren't anywhere close to getting married—or even engaged.

Still, she wondered why he wanted to buy the ranch. For some reason, she didn't peg Ty for the type of person who was...responsible enough to do such a thing. She bit down on the thought. Determination to take the thought to the grave dove through her. She would not hurt Ty with such a comment.

They sat side by side as the floats went by, as the cheerleaders did backflips, as the fire truck blew its horn, only separated by a couple of feet. But a chasm existed between them, and River didn't even know when it had formed.

———

Ty wiped the sweat from his forehead before settling his hat back in place. Lexi and Hannah had gotten twenty tickets each, and he wondered how much longer he could possibly walk around the carnival in this heat.

River Lee looked close to melting—and to melting down. He'd never seen her so frustrated with her kids, and he had absolutely no idea what to do to help her. If she'd even want his help. His own patience dangled at the end of a very thin rope, and he detoured toward the freshly squeezed lemonade stand as they made their way back over to the jungle cruisers for the third time.

"Be right there," he told River Lee and she nodded to acknowledge that she'd heard him. He watched her for a few seconds, enjoying the curve in her hips, the length in her legs. Everything else about today had been a complete bust.

He wasn't sure how he'd expected River Lee to react to his news about the ranch, but cold disbelief wasn't it. He'd been in to see Vic Stansfield at the bank twice now, trying to secure the funding he needed for the ranch.

It hadn't gone well either time. Ty had virtually no assets. No home of his own. The truck he drove belonged to the ranch. The most expensive thing he owned was his three-hundred-dollar cowboy hat, and well, that didn't go very far as collateral for a ranch that cost well into seven-figure territory.

A lump pressed against his windpipe. He really wanted Horseshoe Home. He *needed* it. Needed to be able to provide a stable life and a steady income for River Lee and her girls. He couldn't imagine her living with him in his one-bedroom cowboy cabin, and he certainly couldn't move into her mother's basement.

"Two, please," he told the girl when it was his turn to order. The constant wrestling sessions with himself left him exhausted and moody, both things he didn't quite know how to deal with.

He paid for his refreshments and turned to find River Lee. His eyes landed on Jace and Belle, each of them holding one of their son's hands as they waited in line for the carousel. And in that moment, that single snapshot of life, Ty knew he wouldn't get the ranch.

As if God himself had parted the clouds and shouted into Ty's soul, he knew that Jace would buy it. Knew that Jace had been to the bank too. Knew that Jace had more to his name than a pair of boots and a cowboy hat.

Bitterness Ty didn't know how to swallow coated his mouth. And he hated it. Hated that he felt this way about one of his best friends. Hated that he couldn't be happy for the man who'd also worked his entire life in the fields of Horseshoe Home.

He tore his gaze from the little family, his grip on the lemonade cups almost crushing them. He eased up as he spotted River Lee leaning against the trunk of a tree as she kept an eye on her girls.

"Here you go." He gave her the best smile he could muster up, which surely didn't amount to much. She didn't return it, but the grateful look in her eyes and the way she sighed after she took a long drink of the lemonade broadcasted her relief.

"I think I'm gonna go," he said.

"You are?" Her eyebrows lifted and she started choking the lemonade cup. "I thought we were gonna go to the dance together tonight."

"That's not for hours, sweetheart." He leaned down and pressed a kiss to her forehead, his cowboy hat getting bumped back on his head. He adjusted it and added, "I'm tired and sweaty, and I think I'm gonna go on home and shower before the dance."

He didn't ask if that was okay with her. Truth was, he'd probably saddle Abracadabra and ride up the hillside. He needed something to anchor himself to, and while he'd hoped River Lee would provide that solid spot, her reaction to his proclamation about buying the ranch hadn't been what he'd hoped.

"All right," she said. "I've got to get the girls home and down for naps anyway."

"Of course." Ty fell back a step, the lemonade making everything in him sour. Or maybe that was his jealous heart sending shockwaves of saltiness through him. "I'll see you later." He turned and wove himself into the crowd so she wouldn't be able to see the emotion he felt sure showed on his face.

Emotion he wished he didn't have. He couldn't believe he was jealous of a five-year-old. And he wasn't really jealous. Just...uncertain. Unsure of where he belonged in River Lee's life.

If he belonged in River Lee's life.

———

By the time Ty returned to Gold Valley, he'd taken his horse all the way to the northeast cabin, where they'd both rested in the shade for an hour before making the trip back to the ranch. He'd avoided speaking with Caleb, or Jace, or anyone else as he brushed down the animal and hurried back to his cabin. Behind the closed door, he'd exhaled like he hadn't been breathing properly all day.

He approached Kevin, the supervisor for volunteers, feeling a bit out of place in the central square though he'd been there every weekend this summer. Though he'd had a partner in River Lee.

"Where do you want me to start?"

Kevin glanced up from the clipboard he carried. He smiled when he recognized Ty. "Dance floor. Rory called in and said he can't come, so I'll need your muscles on that."

"You got it, boss." Ty stepped past the other man and headed for the moving van where Kevin kept the removable dance floor when it wasn't laid over the grass in the central square. He hauled box after box of tiles from the van, the labor something he understood, something he didn't have to think about.

And he needed something he could do without having to expend so much mental energy. Because heaven knew he didn't have a brain cell to spare, as many as he spent on River Lee, his future, the possibility of spending it with her, all of it.

By the time the floor was laid, Ty was as sweaty as he'd been that afternoon and just as confused as ever.

Especially when River didn't arrive by nine-thirty, when he expected her to.

CHAPTER 15

*H*alf an hour later, Ty paced behind the refreshment table, his feelings becoming more raw by the moment. He needed to leave. Needed to escape back to the ranch, where no one could see he'd been stood up. Needed some time to figure out why he felt like he'd been pierced through the heart with River Lee's absence.

"Hey, can I take off?" he asked Kevin when he couldn't stand around solo for another second.

"Sure thing, Ty. Thanks for your help."

"You can manage the floor?"

"We're going to leave it since the weekend dance is only two days away."

Ty nodded, his throat tight, tight. "I won't be able to come down on Saturday," he managed to say. He didn't want to lie, so he didn't say why. He wouldn't be able to come down, simple as that.

Kevin's eyes hooked onto Ty's and understanding flowed between them. They weren't particularly good friends; Kevin was at least a decade older than Ty. But the man wasn't stupid, and surely he'd seen Ty twirling River Lee around the dance floor and then disappearing into the night.

"All right," Kevin said, his words drawn out. "Everything okay?"

"A-okay," Ty said, forcing his lips to curve upward. Smiling had never felt so hard, and Ty gave up trying after two seconds. He ducked his head and set his feet walking.

Halfway to his truck, his phone buzzed. He almost didn't pull it out to check it. But in the end, he couldn't just ignore it, because he knew it would be River Lee.

Sure enough, she'd texted to ask if he was still awake.

Annoyance sang through him. Did she think he was home in bed? *Why* would she think that? He didn't even know how to respond, so he stuffed his phone in his back pocket and climbed into the truck.

He felt like he was suffocating, and he hurried to roll the windows down and get the truck in gear. The air flow though the cab didn't seem to help that much, and he yanked the wheel to the left to enter the parking lot at the waterfalls.

The roar of them floated on the air though he couldn't see the falls through the darkness. He realized the absence of the moon at the same time he stepped from the truck. He could see enough to get down the boardwalk, and though he believed he could navigate the trails up to the meadows, he stopped at the end of the path.

He leaned against the railing and stared toward the waterfalls, angry at himself for falling so far so fast with River Lee. Angry with her for not coming tonight. Angry with God for letting her leave Gold Valley in the first place.

He held onto the irritation, the fury, for several long breaths. Then he exhaled them all into the atmosphere. He never was one to hang onto things that brought him down. It simply felt like several weights had been added to his shoulders in a very short period of time.

River Lee, her girls, the ranch.

But most of all, River Lee.

———

River gripped her phone in her fist, willing Ty to answer her. When another minute passed and he stayed silent, she thumbed out *Hannah wasn't feeling well and I couldn't get away tonight.*

She should just call him, make sure he was okay. That *they* were okay.

River's stomach writhed and the bones in her fingers ached. She released them and practically punched the call button, determined to talk to him before the night ended.

He didn't pick up, which only made her blood boil harder. She didn't wait for his voice mail to finish before she ended the call and opened another one.

"Hello?" he asked as if he didn't know who was calling,

as if she hadn't texted several times and just called literally five seconds ago.

"Hello?" she mimicked. "What's going on?"

"What's goin' on?" he threw back at her. "What do you think is goin' on?" The bite in his tone wasn't hard to hear. Neither was the wind coming through the line, which meant he was driving.

"You're mad I didn't come to the dance." River cocked her hip and looked out the kitchen window and into the beautiful backyard.

"I'm not mad," he said, but he certainly sounded mad.

"Well, what are you, then?"

"Disappointed," he said after several seconds of silence. "Frustrated."

A stab of pain bolted through River's head, right behind her eyes. "I'm sorry." Her voice sounded like a wounded bird. "Hannah was—"

"Sick," he said. "I know."

When he didn't add anything else, hopelessness filled River. Her mind had been playing tricks on her all afternoon, and she couldn't figure out how to shake the nagging feeling that Ty was more than disappointed she hadn't come to the dance.

"You didn't like the carnival this afternoon, did you?" she asked.

"It was just hot."

"You're not a very good liar." She forced a laugh through her lips, but it didn't sound right. "You never were."

"Just something I'm working through."

"Did you get through it?"

"No."

"What is it? Maybe I can help."

"Nope," he said. "You can't, and I don't want to tell you."

"Ty—"

"River Lee, I'll figure it out, but I'm not talking about it right now."

Tears threatened to stain her cheeks and infuse her voice. "I should've called earlier," she said. "I lost track of time, that's all. Hannah—she—she just needed me, and we sort of dozed on the couch. It got late, and I didn't realize it."

"It's fine, River Lee."

But it wasn't fine, and she could hear it in every syllable of her name. "I'm not working tomorrow," she said. "Do you want to meet for lunch?"

"I do," he said. "But I probably won't be able to make that. Cowboys don't get days off."

"You didn't work today."

"Oh, but I did. We were all up before dawn to get chores done so we could get down to the parade."

River turned away from the window, at a loss. She didn't know or understand Ty's life. She did know he was hiding something from her.

"I'll call you later, okay? I'm about to lose service."

"Okay, but—" She swallowed and gathered her courage. "Call me if you can make lunch. I'd really like to see you."

"I'll let you know." The line went dead and River hoped

Ty had driven through that dead spot and not hung up on her.

She had a hard time sleeping that night, and she loathed every moment that passed the following morning where Ty didn't call. She wore a path in the carpet from the front door to the linoleum in the kitchen until her mother said, "River Lee, you're makin' me nervous. Go talk to Ty."

River tossed her mother a disgruntled look. "How do I do that, Mom? Just drive up to the ranch and...and then what?" The idea tumbled through her mind, gaining momentum the longer she entertained it.

"I don't know, but if you keep walking back and forth like that, I'm going to lose my mind." She tossed River a disgruntled look. "Come on, girls. Let's get to our movie."

Her mother had signed up the girls for a summer movie every Thursday morning, something to get them out of the house, give them something to do. River watched her mother get shoes on the girls and hustle them out the door.

Discomfort threaded through River, and she grabbed her purse from the table and followed her mother out the door. Her destination was quite a bit farther than the movie theater, but she kept on toward the ranch, her determination outweighing her fear for maybe the first time in her life.

She almost missed the turnoff to the ranch, and she thought her car would bounce right off the gravel road that led to the row of cowboy cabins. Pickup trucks sat everywhere, and as River got out of her car, three cowboys came down the front steps of the second largest house on the property.

River's wits abandoned her and her flight instinct urged her back to the car. Thankfully, her feet seemed to have frozen to the ground. She didn't recognize any of the men moving closer to her.

"Ma'am." One cowboy tipped his hat. "Can we help you?"

"I'm—" She cleared her throat. "I'm looking for Ty Barker."

"Sure." The man glanced back the way he'd come. "He's in the admin lodge with Caleb."

River's heart dropped to her feet and rebounded into the wrong spot in her chest. She had to face Ty and Caleb at the same time? She smoothed her palms down the front of her blouse and gave the three cowboys in front of her a curt nod. "Thank you."

Every step toward the lodge caused River's pulse to double. She thought sure the organ would burst from behind her ribs before she could gain the top of the stairs. The door barely moved when she leaned her full weight into it, but she finally got it open.

Before her, a large room held desks and chairs. Laughter and chatter bubbled out of a doorway directly across from her, but she'd have to weave through the maze of desks to get there. So weave she did.

A hallway stretched to her left, but she poked her head into the doorway to find a kitchen filled with long tables—a break room of sorts. Several cowboys sat at the tables, but only one captured River's attention.

Ty stood, his dark cowboy hat not quite shielding the surprise in his hazel eyes. "River Lee?" he drawled, drawing the attention of every man in the room to her.

"Can I talk to you for a second?" she asked.

Ty didn't move. Didn't twitch. Didn't blink.

"Go on," Caleb said with a heavy dose of amusement in his voice. "The woman drove all the way out here. You can give her *one second*."

Ty sent a scowl in Caleb's direction that mirrored the way River felt. He marched toward her and she backed out of the doorway as he approached, the stormy expression on his face anything but settling.

"C'mon," he muttered as he squeezed past her. She hoped he'd take her hand, claim her as his, but he didn't. With little choice, she followed him around the maze of desks and back out into the sunshine. The loss of the air conditioning was almost as painful as Ty's treatment of her.

"Can you slow down?" she asked as he practically flew down the steps and across the yard.

Ty glanced over his shoulder like he'd just realized she was there. His step slowed, and she caught him before slipping her fingers between his. "I'm sorry about the dance."

He exhaled, his eyes searching the sky for something, but there wasn't even so much as a cloud in sight. "This has nothing to do with the dance," he finally said.

At least he'd spoken the truth. River took a deep breath of the fresh country air. "What does it have to do with?"

CHAPTER 16

*R*iver kept walking, wondering when Ty would stop. But she didn't want to say anything else. Not until he did. Not until he was ready to tell her what was eating him.

Besides, she'd already said enough. *Just tell me. We'll work it out.*

And then, *I don't see how it can be worse than anything else that's happened to me recently.*

And her personal nemesis, one she'd wished she could take back as soon as she'd said it: *I drove all the way out here. The least you can do is talk to me.*

He'd bristled at that, and bristled hard. He hadn't invited her to the ranch. He hadn't wanted to talk to her, that much had been obvious from their conversation the previous evening. But her mother had said....

River shaded her eyes with her free hand. "So now that I've been here for several weeks, and my job is going pretty well, I've decided to buy a house. Make my life here permanent."

Ty grunted but didn't offer anything more.

"And wouldn't you know it? My mom's new boyfriend used to be a realtor. His license is still valid, so he's helping me." She avoided a large rock in the trail, taking her farther from Ty.

"I first thought about getting one of those new houses on the northwest side of town. You know, where Sterling Maughan lives?"

"I know it." Ty's words clipped from his mouth.

"But they were too big for me." She added a giggle to her statement, even though she felt anything but carefree. "And too expensive." River gave him a few beats to add something —anything—to the conversation, but he didn't.

Her patience stretched, and she employed everything she did when she was dealing with her three-year-old. "So I'm going to be looking at something a little smaller and in an older neighborhood." She resisted the urge to check her phone for the time. "A little later this afternoon."

They reached a fork in the trail, one leg heading further up the mountain and the other heading further into the trees. "Well, I can see I'm bothering you. Keeping you from your work." River turned around, prepared to get back to the ranch on her own. "Call me later."

She'd taken three steps when he said, "I feel inadequate."

River faced him, confusion coursing through her. He was anything but inadequate. "About what?"

Ty looked at her, every emotion laid open on his face. "I feel inadequate to be your boyfriend."

———

Ty swallowed hard, the words surging against the back of his tongue about to spill out and stain everything. River Lee tipped her head back and laughed. Laughed like he'd said the funniest thing on the planet. Laughed like she had when they were younger, when they were more carefree.

She sobered when he didn't join in and cocked her hip. "That is the most ridiculous thing I've ever heard."

"Is it?" he challenged. "If this—" He gestured between them. "Becomes serious—and I'm not sayin' it's not already serious. But let's say it gets serious enough that we, I don't know, get married."

River Lee flinched at his last word, but he plowed on. "Then what, River Lee? You're gonna come live with me in my one-bedroom cowboy cabin? Or I'm gonna move into your mother's basement?"

Her blue eyes flashed fire and then ice. Cold, cold ice. "I just said I was looking to buy a house of my own."

"I don't make enough to support a family." Pure anguish raced through him, and he gritted his teeth to keep it inside. He didn't want to show this weakness, not to her. Not to anyone.

"Ty." She stepped into him and wrapped her arms around him. He remained stiff and unyielding—at least until she skated her fingernails along the back of his neck.

Then he relaxed into her embrace and did what he'd been dying to do since he saw her framed in that doorway in the administration lodge. He took a deep breath of the soft, floral scent of her skin, his tension draining away.

She chuckled, the vibrations in her chest shaking against his. "I can't believe you—the non-serious single cowboy—has been thinking so hard about the future."

"Hey." He wasn't exactly hurt, but he hadn't exactly thought about marriage with anyone else either. "It's just… you have two kids, River Lee. I—I like you a lot, and I—" He had no idea how to finish his thought, so he just let it hang in the air between them.

She peered up at him, waiting for him to go on. Instead, he leaned down and touched his lips to hers. There one moment, gone the next. Even with a kiss so fast, he still felt stronger about her than any woman he'd ever dated.

"I was scared," he whispered.

"Is that why you wanted to buy the ranch?"

"I thought it would give you some stability." He gazed over her shoulder, back toward the ranch they'd left behind. "But that won't happen. I can't get the funding I need. Jace will end up buying it."

"You'll still have a job, right?"

"Yeah, I'll probably become the general controller, even. Me and Caleb think Jace will buy the ranch, and then he'll need a new foreman, of course. He can't own the ranch and be the foreman. Caleb takes care of the herd, all the agricultural stuff, but he could become foreman. If not, I might get the job. Or Nelson, who's the general controller.

If that happens, I could maybe take his job as the controller."

"Sounds complicated." River Lee smiled, something Ty wanted to witness every day of his life.

"It's not," Ty said. "Very little about ranching is. Although, Caleb did say he wasn't sure he wanted to be foreman. Too much paperwork, and he'd need to hire someone to oversee the agricultural side of the ranch, which he loves."

River Lee tucked herself into Ty's side and gently guided him back down the path. "So you'll have a job, and a place to live, and an amazing girlfriend."

Ty chuckled. "I suppose so." He wondered what he'd been so worried about. "If I don't live on the ranch, I'll probably get a housing allowance."

River Lee said, "All right," and stepped, stepped, stepped. "And you know, Ty, I'm not looking to get married right away. I mean, don't get me wrong, I like you. I just—"

"Need more time," he said.

"Right," she said. "Time. I have a lot going on in my life, and I'm probably going to move soon, and Lexi will be starting kindergarten, and we don't need to rush things."

"Of course not." But the thought left Ty hollow inside. The thought of living through the bitter temperatures of another winter alone made his bones ache. At the same time, he wasn't in love with River Lee—yet—and he still needed to figure out how to deal with his place in line behind Lexi and Hannah.

They arrived back at the ranch, where River Lee said,

"So I guess lunch is out." She wasn't asking, and her tone suggested she was teasing him.

"Sorry, River Lee." He didn't know what else to say. "I do have to get back to work, but I'll see you on Saturday morning, okay?"

She stretched up to kiss him, and he gladly complied, taking his time to convey his feelings for her, his apology for freaking out about a future that was as uncertain as it had always been. She matched his intensity, encouraging Ty to maintain the contact—and get out of his own head so he didn't mess things up with River Lee.

CHAPTER 17

*T*y spent his early mornings riding up to check the herd. His afternoons trying to stay cool by working on the machinery or hauling hay. It was almost harvest time, and that meant the Harvest Festival was just around the corner.

He drove down to the valley in the evenings for planning meetings, or sat on his front porch and sent texts and made phone calls. He and River Lee met to plan the Huck Finn fishing event, and he spent the entire day with her that Saturday. Horseback riding lessons, lunch, planning, and another walk to the duck pond pushed him closer and closer to falling in love with her.

And the way she kissed him suggested she was falling for him too.

He didn't bring it up. He didn't tell her he loved her. Didn't mention their future again.

A few days before the Harvest Festival, Jace burst into

the administration lodge during lunch time. "It's official, boys," he said, a giant grin on his face. "As of January first, I'll be the new owner of Horseshoe Home Ranch."

A cheer went up, and Ty joined in. He'd searched for a way to be happy for his friend, and God had granted him the ability to feel Jace's joy as if it were his own. A sense of gratitude filled him again. Gratitude that he was able to participate in Jace's happiness. Gratitude that he could find joy even if he didn't get what he thought he wanted.

The Lord works in mysterious ways, he thought as the festivities died down. Jace moved through the crowd, headed for his office. Ty met him at the mouth of the hallway and pumped the foreman's hand. "Congratulations, Jace. You and Belle will be real good owners."

Jace nodded him down the hall, and Ty followed him into his office. "I heard you wanted to buy the ranch."

Ty scrubbed the back of his head at the seriousness in Jace's voice. Though the man was only a few years older than he was, Ty viewed him as almost a father figure. "I couldn't get the funding. I don't actually own anything and don't even use a credit card."

"You want to run the ranch?"

Ty lifted his gaze to Jace's. "I don't know."

"You don't know?"

His mind whirled, whizzed, wove through possibilities. "I—"

Jace exhaled and moved behind his desk. He said, "I also heard you've been datin' River Lee Whitely," as he sat.

"Yeah." Ty grinned, unable to keep the gesture from his face. "We like each other."

Jace chuckled. "So the foreman's cabin is big enough for a family. Things that serious with River Lee?"

"Not quite," Ty said. "Hopefully, though."

"So you like her a lot."

Ty shrugged. "Yeah, sure, I like her a lot." He spoke true, but as soon as the words left his mouth, he realized he had more than like in his life for River Lee. He had a little bit of love for her. "She just bought a house," Ty said. "She's movin' at the end of the month."

"Well, no one wants to get married in the winter," Jace said as he pulled a folder toward him. "Believe me, I would know."

Ty laughed and watched Jace get to work. "So is this what the foreman does?" He glanced around the office, not quite sure how he felt about sitting behind a desk, behind these walls.

"It's not always a picnic," Jace said. "Make no mistake about that." He glanced up and met Ty's eye. "I'll be choosing the foreman by the end of the month, so I can train him before I take ownership. Do you want me to consider you?"

"Does the foreman have to live on-site?"

"It's easier," Jace said. "It's not a nine-to-five job, Ty."

Ty glanced around the office again. Gray walls. Curtains with gray and white chevrons. A picture of Jace and Belle on their wedding day sat on the desk, the only personal touch he'd added to the office.

He'd make more as the foreman. Have a bigger house. Maybe River Lee would move up here with him if they got married.

"I want to be considered, boss."

Jace went back to work. "All right, then. I'll let you know."

Ty backed out of the office and then turned back. "Remember I'll be gone on Thursday, Friday, and Saturday for Harvest Days."

"I remember," Jace said without looking up.

"Who else are you considering for the foreman job?"

"Everyone." A bit of annoyance accompanied the word, and Ty took his cue to get out of there before he blew his chance at the job completely.

———

River left work at lunchtime on Thursday, glad she could close the folders containing the cases of her charges. The girls were only going to be at Silver Creek for another week, and she thought several of them had made real progress.

The pride she felt expanded and then evaporated. She'd fumbled around for weeks before figuring out the intricacies of her job, and any progress these girls had made certainly wasn't because of her. The group leaders worked ten times harder than she did, and every girl on River's list had talked about how much they loved the horses.

If there was one thing River didn't understand, it was that. She'd suffered through the last eleven weeks of horseback riding lessons, and the last lesson couldn't get over fast enough. Even though the Harvest Festival would be in full swing on Saturday morning, Ty hadn't canceled the lesson. Claimed Silver Creek needed to stay on schedule with such things.

He had moved the time to earlier in the day so everyone could attend the parade in the morning. A sour taste filled River's mouth. She didn't want to repeat the Fourth of July parade and following carnival. In fact, she'd taken steps to ensure the Harvest Festival turned out much better than July's event.

Ty had bought tickets to the rodeo for Saturday night, and she'd taken the girls to the carnival after the children's parade the previous day. She parked in her mother's driveway and hurried into the house. "Lexi, Hannah. It's time to go if you want to catch some fish."

The girls came rushing down the hall from their bedroom, both of them wearing their swimming suits and carrying towels. Her mother followed them, rubbing her hands together. "I just put sunscreen on them."

River hugged her mother. "Thanks, Mom. Let's go girls." They filled the car with their girlish chatter and giggles, and River drove them all to Battlecreek Park, where the parking lot was already full.

She parked down the street and herded the girls toward the crowd. She passed the girls to her friend, Jodi, who had a five-year-old daughter and lived down the street from

River's mother. "I'll be at the registration table." She flashed a smile at Jodi. "Thanks so much."

Jodi, a dark-haired stay-at-home mom had also offered to babysit the girls, walk Lexi to kindergarten, and even brought dinner to River one night. It had been a fast friendship, which River really appreciated now, as she made her way through the long line to begin her first real community service.

Ty was already seated at the table, his sexy cowboy hat perched on his head. "Sure, Suzy Curtis," he drawled as he searched a paper in front of him. "Here you are, Suzy." He made a checkmark next to a name and handed the girl a sticker. "That goes somewhere on your swim suit. You can take two fish home, all right?"

The mother thanked Ty and moved out of line.

River slid into the chair next to him. "Okay, so I just check them off and give them a sticker?" She examined the list in front of her. "I thought registration opened at three."

"Hey, beautiful." Ty flashed her a smile. "She was the first one I did. You just find them, check them off, give them the sticker. They're colored coordinated and numbered so not everyone goes in at once. No sticker, no admission to the pond. Kids can take two fish home. Easy as pie."

"Only if it's peach pie," River quipped and turned her attention to the woman standing with three boys.

Ty's soft laughter reached her ears, and she wished this whole Huck Finn event was over so they could go to dinner, hold hands, talk about their future.

He hadn't said anything more about his fears or their future since the Fourth of July. River suspected he was waiting for her to bring it up, but she didn't quite know how.

"I close next weekend," River said as she waited while the boys stuck their stickers to their swim shorts. "I'm moving the weekend after that. Can I borrow your truck and your muscles?"

"Always usin' me for my body," he joked under his breath.

A smile exploded across River's face. "And that truck. Don't forget about that."

He looked at her, his green-brown eyes hooking into her blue ones and holding on. A moment passed between them. A moment full of heat. A moment where River thought she could spend the rest of her life with this man.

She ducked her head and raised her eyes to the next person in line. "Name?"

As she searched for the name on the list, Ty's fingers brushed hers. Could've been an innocent touch to any watching, but River knew it was more than that. He couldn't wait until their time alone tonight either.

———

"I got two fish!" Lexi kept saying. Over and over.

River said, "Mm hmm," for at least the tenth time, her blood flowing through her body like it contained live electricity. She'd planned to take the girls with her to dinner with Ty, but now that the hour had arrived, she didn't want to.

She loved her girls. She did. She didn't want to choose a man over them, but if it had been John, she'd have chosen him over Lexi and Hannah. Their relationship was supposed to last longer than the girls would be in the house. Their marriage was what had started the family in the first place.

River pulled into the driveway at her mom's house, the stench of fish and pond water filling her nostrils. "Baths," she told the girls. "Then we're going to dinner with Mister Ty."

Hannah and Lexi piled out of the car, still chattering about the fish and the pond and the butterflies they'd chased while they waited for the green group to be called. River watched them climb the steps and enter the house, a smile drifting across her lips.

Yes, she wanted to spend time alone with Ty, but her mother also had a date that night, and her girls were River's responsibility. She thought briefly of calling Jodi to watch them, but reminded herself that Jodi had already helped her for hours that day.

In the end, she heaved herself out of the car too and went to freshen up for dinner with Ty. As she curled her hair and added a fresh layer of lip gloss in anticipation of seeing her boyfriend, River's mind drifted to the future.

She'd caught herself doing it from time to time after

John left. He'd kept paying for the house, everything the girls needed, all of it—until everything with the custody was settled.

Then he'd told her he'd pay the child support and alimony—and that wasn't enough to keep the house in Vegas without finding a job. River had opted to return to Gold Valley, where she had help, could afford cheaper housing, and a job had just opened up.

Now that she was here, settled into her job well enough, and had bought a house, River's future centered around her relationship with Ty.

Only three more weeks, she thought, pausing in her grooming. *Three more weeks until you would've left for college.*

She shook her head at her teenage self, wishing she could go back in time and tell her eighteen-year-old self not to leave town, not to leave Ty. He'd given her every indication that their relationship would continue well into autumn, way past winter. Every time he sat by her in church and held her hand, she felt like they'd be doing that every week until their hair turned white and their skin wrinkled. Such peace, such happiness, had never coursed through her so strongly.

Every time he called, or texted, or sent her a smile—even if it was during the dreaded horseback riding lessons—she couldn't help the leap her pulse took. Such things had died when John graduated from law school and began clocking eighty-hour weeks. River knew ranching required long hours, but she couldn't imagine Ty choosing the job over his wife and children. Of course, maybe she didn't know him as well as she thought. She of all people knew that a wedding changed a lot more than a woman's last name.

"C'mon girls." River turned from the mirror, from her internal thoughts, and knelt to help her girls wash the fish stink from their hair. She barely had them dressed and their hair in ponytails before Ty knocked on the front door, pushing it open a moment later.

"Hey, Mister Ty!" Lexi called from the barstool where River still worked on her hair. She tried to get down, but River put her hand on her shoulder.

"Wait a second, baby. I need to spray it." By the time she'd hairsprayed Lexi's hair, Ty had walked into the kitchen.

He pressed a kiss to River's temple along with the whispered, "Wow, you look great," before turning his attention to the girls. He exclaimed over their hair and their matching plaid shirts and asked if they liked pizza more than pasta.

As River tucked the comb and hairspray back into the hair bag, her heart swelled with love. Love for Ty.

Horror struck her right in the throat, but it fled in the next heartbeat.

"River Lee?"

She startled at the proximity of Ty, at the intense way he peered at her. "Yeah." She smoothed her hair, trying to find her center. "Yes, I'm ready to go."

"You girls go load into the car," Ty said, gently pushing the girls toward the front door. As they went, he swept his hands around her waist and brought her close, close. "You smell fantastic." He slid his lips along her jaw, down the column of her neck. "And it's criminal to wear shorts like that when we won't be alone for hours."

Warmth filled her at the same time his cowboy hat hit the floor. Heat exploded through her when he finally claimed her lips, and River gave herself completely to the feel, touch, and kiss of this man.

CHAPTER 18

River pulled the tape gun over the flaps of the box and ran her hand down the side. "There. That's the last one." She stood and stretched her back, amazed she'd been able to pack everything of hers and her girls in only two days.

Of course, her back was paying a heavy price, but she'd rather work for twenty hours straight than live in a sea of boxes.

"Knock, knock." Ty's voice filtered down the hall and spurred River into motion.

"Down here," she called and stepped out of the bedroom. She drank in the sight of him in his jeans, that belt buckle and cowboy hat, his blue, short-sleeved shirt. His muscles flexed as he smiled and drew her into an embrace.

"Moving day," he murmured.

"Moving day," she confirmed, a blast of nerves hitting her. She wasn't sure why. Maybe because she'd never purchased a house on her own before. She and John had rented until he finished law school, and they'd bought their house on the east side of Vegas together.

"So." He exhaled, stepped back, and glanced into the bedroom. "How much are we lookin' at?"

"Not much," she said. "I sold all my furniture before coming here. We only have boxes of clothes, some kitchen stuff, little things."

He edged past her and scanned the bedroom fully now. "This alone will fill my truck."

"Kids have a lot of stuff."

"This your room?" He nodded down the hall.

"Yes."

He cast her one last look before moving that way. He whistled. "*Women* have a lot of stuff."

She laughed, the merriment in the sound pure and absolutely thrilling to her. She hadn't been this happy in two years, since she discovered her husband's infidelity, since he'd refused the marriage counseling.

She quieted and found Ty leaning against her bedroom doorframe, a silly smile on his face. Still, it could light a fireworks show, and she found herself returning the grin. "What?"

"I like it when you laugh."

"Stop it." She turned away and slipped into the girls' bedroom to pick up a box.

"Stop what?" He came up behind her, his cologne making her head swim a little. Her grip on the box slipped and she righted it.

"Making fun of my laugh."

He stacked two boxes and lifted them. "I wasn't making fun of it." He gave her that heated look that made her stomach feel like marshmallows. "I really do like it." He left her in the wake of his masculinity, his cowboy boots striding down the hall and out the front door.

River tucked her hair behind her ear and tried not to find him so attractive. But it wasn't just that. She was holding onto the edge of a cliff, her fingers scrabbling for purchase, her strength to keep herself from falling all the way in love with Ty failing her.

He returned as if summoned by her thoughts. "Hey, you game to go to the church fundraiser with me next weekend? The ranch is donating five bull calves, and I'm bringin' 'em down."

"Only in Montana could you auction off bull calves to raise money for a church."

Ty scoffed. "Not true. I'm sure they do it in Texas too. Utah maybe." He picked up two more boxes and flashed her a grin that made her knees go weak. "You gonna bring that box out to the truck or just stand there lookin' pretty?"

"Just stand here," she called after him, eliciting another chuckle. A vein of delight squirreled down her spine and she followed Ty outside to his truck.

"Hey, River," Jodi said. "You remember my husband Jason."

"Of course." River handed the box to Ty and then introduced him to her friends. "They're keeping the girls while we move today."

Ty shook hands with both of them and laced his fingers through River's. "Thanks for your help." He focused one of his grins on them, and Jodi practically swooned. River stifled her giggle and tucked her arm around Ty's waist.

"Well, let's not waste Jodi's generosity."

Jodi scoffed at the same time she extended a bag of cookies toward River. "Fresh-baked. I told Hannah she could help with something later today."

"Oh, how sweet. Thank you." River accepted the cookies as her mother exited the house with a box and a very pronounced sniffle.

River exchanged a glance with Ty, said, "Excuse me," to Jodi and Jason, and went to intercept her mother.

"Mom, I'm moving less than two miles away."

She nodded, short little bursts of movement. "I'm just gonna miss you, that's all."

"I know." River took the box and handed it off to Ty. She hugged her mom. "You'll see me everyday. You're my babysitter, remember?"

Her mom wiped her eyes. "I know." She gave a half-laugh, half-sob. "I'm being silly."

"You'll have more time to spend with Milton."

"You're right. And I know you need to be on your own."

River nodded, empathy passing through her. "Love you, Mom." She turned away as her own emotions snuck up on her. She didn't truly have any sadness about leaving her mother's house. Her daughters could make new friends in her new neighborhood, and the town wasn't that big. She'd see Jodi at church, just like she always did.

And River liked going to lunch with her girlfriends just fine.

"All right." She wiped her hands on her shorts. "Another box."

Several hours later, she lay on the second-hand couch Jodi had given her, every muscle in her body protesting all movement. Ty held his phone to his ear, ordering food for dinner as she'd complained she didn't have the energy to go out.

"Your mom's keepin' the girls overnight." Ty lifted her ankles and sat on the couch, repositioning her legs across his lap. "Chinese food is on the way." He glanced around as River let her eyes drift closed. "I can't believe you moved everything and then unpacked it all in one day."

"Not all of it." She pointed lazily into the kitchen, where four packed boxes still sat on the counter. She had no kitchen table, no bar stools. But she had a bed for herself and one for the girls, and she had enough to shower, get ready, go to work, and order pizza until she felt up to unpacking the dishes and cookware.

Ty started rubbing her feet, and a moan of pleasure escaped her throat. "You've had a long day," he said quietly, his strength and steadiness so alluring. "But I have some news to share with you."

She opened her eyes, her interest piqued. "Go on, then." He looked like a little boy on Christmas morning, his smile the thing that lit the lights on the tree.

"Jace gave me the foreman job."

River sat up and flung her arms around Ty, squeezing

him tight. "That's great, Ty." She skated her lips down the side of his face in search of his mouth. When she found it, she formed her lips to hers and kissed him congratulations.

After several long moments, he chuckled. "I wanna have good news every day," he said, his voice a bit scratchy. Definitely sexy.

She kissed him again, letting go of the ledge she'd been holding onto and letting herself fall all the way in love with Ty Barker.

———

Ty started every day in Jace's office, an hour later than he usually went up to the range. Though he was getting more sleep, he didn't have as much energy as he used to. He wanted to start the day with the sunrise not a folder detailing the supplies the ranch needed or the nutritional needs of the cattle for the upcoming winter. And the Thursday payroll was torture, just like Jace had said it'd be.

But Ty didn't mind so much. Sure, he thought week after week of Thursday payroll would take it's toll, but for now, Ty was just excited to be doing something different, learning something new.

"You'll want to spend time getting to know the men," Jace said one morning near the end of September. "Talk to them, work alongside them, never act like you're higher than them." He moved down the row of troughs, dropping the purifying pellets the cattle needed. Ty followed him with the testing kit to make sure the pH was correct.

With winter approaching, everything on the ranch had switched into high gear. The harvest was almost in, with cowboys heading out to the fields from dawn until dark, which made for a thirteen-hour work day. Jace had taught Ty how to rotate the men through the shifts so that they only worked their eight hours, but the efficiency of their time stayed at its peak.

Jace reached the end of the row and turned back to Ty. "Let's go check in with Caleb."

A flurry of nerves swarmed Ty's chest. "How's he doin' with all this?" Caleb hadn't acted any different during lunchtime, but Ty's available minutes to sit around and eat had seriously dwindled.

"He's just fine," Jace said. "He didn't put in for foreman." He cut Ty a quick glance out of the corner of his eye. "Six others did, but Caleb wasn't one of them."

Surprise traveled through Ty. "He didn't? But he would've gotten it."

"Probably," Jace said. "He started here the year before you; he has seniority; he's a great cowboy."

"Why didn't he put in for foreman?"

Jace pushed open the feed barn, where they'd find Caleb down in the small office where he worked to keep the cattle healthy.

"Said he didn't want it. Something about how he liked workin' with the herd, usin' his agricultural degree." Jace checked each stall as they passed, but Caleb didn't have any cattle in for testing. "Mornin', Caleb." He leaned in the doorway of Caleb's room, where he leaned over the waist-high table in the corner, studying something.

"Morning." He didn't turn around.

"Ty's here to find out what you do."

"I know what he does." Ty edged into the room too, sweeping the papers tacked to the board above the table. "He manages the nutritional needs of the herd, addresses how to maximize the harvest, that kind of stuff."

Caleb grinned as he turned and leaned his weight into the table. "Yep. That kind of stuff. It only takes a few hours a day, though, so don't take me off other chores."

"Caleb's on a special rotation," Jace said. "And you two will work closely together, so it's important that you know exactly what he does. Not just 'the stuff' you *think* he does."

Ty nodded, the corners of his mouth twitching at the seriousness of Jace. Caleb seemed much more relaxed about the relationship between him and the foreman, but he did point to the page he'd been studying. "Field prep for the winter, so we can reduce the time in the spring it'll take to get the hay in."

The charts seemed written in a different language, but Ty picked them up anyway. "Is this English?" He glanced at Caleb. "This looks like chicken scratch." He chuckled as he tried to make out a word that looked like *scrap metal* but didn't fit with the other words around it.

"Give me those." Caleb snatched the papers away good-naturedly and smoothed them back on the table. "So, you gonna move into the foreman's cabin with River Lee?"

Ty's heart stuttered and seized. He didn't want to talk

about River Lee, not with Jace loitering nearby. He'd just been counseled to get to know his men, and the foreman had ears that were always listening.

"No," Ty said.

"No?" Caleb shifted some papers, but Ty could tell he wasn't looking at them. Not really. "Why not?"

"We're, uh." Ty cleared his throat. "It's not going that fast." He met Jace's eyes. "Plus, Jace said a winter wedding is torture, so there's that too."

Caleb chuckled. "Sometimes you just want to get married, no matter what time of year it is."

"Yeah, sure," Ty said. "But I don't think we're there yet." Ty thought of the last time he'd spent time with River Lee. They'd held hands, talked about the girls, his new job, how things were going in her new house. They shared their lives with each other, and she'd even indicated indirectly that their future would be spent together.

But he hadn't asked about marriage, hadn't mentioned anything to do with diamonds, nothing.

After the girls had gone to bed, there'd been a fair bit of kissing. Kissing that had been passionate, prolonged, and powerful. He let River Lee set the pace, always. He shivered as he remembered the thrill of her fingers in his hair, her legs tangled with his, the heated, slow way she kissed him until she seemed drunk on the taste of him.

"Not there yet?" Caleb asked, incredulity heavy in his voice. "Ty, you've never dated a woman longer than a month. What's this goin' on? Four?"

"About that." Ty folded his arms. "That doesn't mean anything, though."

Caleb abandoned his paperwork and looked squarely at Ty. "Of course it does."

"What does it mean?"

Caleb looked to Jace, almost for permission. Jace lifted one shoulder and studied Ty again. Ty suddenly felt like they'd ganged up on him, that Jace had brought him out here for this conversation and not because of anything to do with the ranch.

"Have you told her you love her yet?" Caleb asked.

Ty scoffed. "I'm not in love with her."

"No?" Jace and Caleb asked together.

Ty volleyed his gaze between the two of them, a significant trapped feeling descending on him. "I—I don't even know what that feels like," he admitted. But if he had to guess, he'd say it was a lot like how he'd felt with River Lee twelve summers ago.

Caleb cocked one eyebrow and turned back to his table. "You'll figure it out."

Jace's radio went off, thank the stars. Nelson's voice came through the speaker with, "Boss, there's a fence down in grid thirteen, and the cattle have crossed the stream."

Jace exhaled heavily as he lifted the radio to his mouth. "I'll send everyone I can." He nodded at Ty. "Let's go."

Ty followed his long stride back down the middle of the barn, back out into the sunshine, back to the business of the ranch. But his mind stayed on the thought of how he felt about River Lee.

He hadn't acknowledged his true feelings for her. Number one, he wasn't sure what they were. Number two, if he admitted how he really felt, he wasn't sure if he could keep the words under his tongue.

He saddled his horse, rode up the mountain to grid thirteen, roped cattle and fixed fences. He went through the physical motions, all the while fighting with himself that he didn't love River Lee.

By the time the day ended, he couldn't deny it any longer.

He was in love with River Lee Whitely, and a smile formed on his face. A smile he couldn't wipe away.

CHAPTER 19

*a*s winter approached, Ty's time with River Lee decreased. She wasn't doing horseback riding lessons anymore, and they didn't have any community service to organize together. He'd see her for a few hours on Saturday afternoons and a few hours at church and afterward.

Ty had been dreaming in diamonds since he'd realized he was in love with River Lee, but he was determined not to bring it up until she did.

As he drove down the canyon with rain pounding his windshield, he wondered if today would be the day she would finally say something. Ever since he'd realized how he felt, he'd been able to sense how much she liked him too. And it was a lot.

The parking lot at the church was practically empty when Ty pulled in, and he wondered if River Lee would brave the weather that morning just to sit by him during a sermon. He took their usual spot about halfway back and shrugged out of his wet leather jacket. He shook out his cowboy hat and had just settled it back onto his head when River Lee slid next to him.

"Hey, cowboy," she said with a heavy dose of flirtation in her voice. She claimed his elbow in both her hands and squeezed. He barely had time to turn toward her before she kissed him.

Shock traveled from the top of his head to his boots at this turn of events. She never kissed him in church, and what he'd said about kissing women in church flowed through his mind. He broke the connection and chuckled, more anxiety in the sound than he liked.

"Where are the girls?"

"They slept over at my mom's, and she didn't want to drive in the rain."

Ty gazed down at her, pure love flowing through him. "River Lee," he whispered.

Her eyes locked on his. "Yeah?"

He swallowed, the words right there, right there, right there. He cleared them from his throat. "Remember what I said about people kissin' in church?"

She blinked, a blip of fear stealing through her eyes. Then her face relaxed and she smiled. "The only people you've seen kiss in church were married or getting married."

"Right." He fidgeted, unable to stop his boots from scraping along the wooden floor. "What do you think about us, you know...." He forced the lump in his throat back down. "About us getting married?"

She searched his face, looking for what he didn't know. He gazed steadily back at her, his heart hammering beneath his breastbone. He slipped his hand into hers and nuzzled her neck. "I'm in love with you, River Lee. I want to marry you."

Her body tensed; her fingers gripped his too tight, too tight.

The organ began to play, and Ty said, "It's okay, River Lee. I'll wait as long as you need." He faced the front, his words almost ripping a hole right through his chest. He breathed deep to contain the emotion, relieved when Dr. Pinnion stood.

River Lee squeezed his fingers and laid her cheek on his bicep. He could feel her happiness, her love, even if she hadn't said anything in words.

———

The week before Halloween, Ty worked in the machinery building, his fingers nearly frozen as he tried to service the engine on a combine.

"Ty, come back," Nelson warbled through the radio.

He pulled his greasy hands from the vehicle and reached for the radio on his belt. "Ty here."

"There's someone on the phone for you, here at the administration lodge."

Ty's brow furrowed. "Who is it?"

"River Taylor."

Ty dropped the wrench he'd been using. "I'm on my way in." He checked his cell as he strode down the path between the barns and stables, the admin lodge suddenly so far away. He had no service, which wasn't that surprising. Horseshoe Home was notorious for having sporadic service beyond the lodge and cabins.

He hurried up the steps and burst into the lodge. Nelson nodded to the phone on the corner of his desk, right there in the middle of the room. Though Ty wanted more privacy, he picked up the phone and waited for Nelson to push the flashing blue button.

"River Lee?" Ty asked. "What's goin' on?" Concern and anxiety spiked. River Lee never called him in the middle of the day. She worked, for one. For two, he called her when he finally got back to his cabin. Every night, like clockwork.

A sniffle came through the line, further alerting Ty to the strange nature of her call. "Tell me what's wrong, sweetheart," he murmured into the line, keeping his back to Nelson and the rest of the room.

She took a deep breath, the sound coming through the line sharp and like a hiss. "I just got off the phone with John."

"All right," Ty said, keeping his voice even and placid. Her ex-husband didn't call a lot, from what she'd told Ty. But he did have two daughters he never saw, and Ty didn't think for a moment that the man would never appear in River Lee's life.

"He's getting remarried in December, and he wants the

girls to be there." Her breath shuddered on the way out. "He wants them for Thanksgiving, and he wants to keep them all the way through the New Year." Her voice finally broke on the last couple of words. After that, only silence came through the line.

Ty didn't know how to respond, not here in this crowded room, not from so far away. "Where are you?" he asked. "At work?"

"Yes." She sounded so broken.

"I'll be there in forty-five minutes." He hung up without waiting for her to confirm and turned back to Nelson. "I have to go down to the valley for the rest of the afternoon. Can you tell Jace?" He pulled his phone from his back pocket. "I have my phone if there's an emergency."

The drive down the canyon seemed to take a lot longer than thirty minutes, every breath agony, every second he couldn't comfort the woman he loved sheer torture.

————

Tears tracked down River's face as she paced in her office. She hugged herself like she could keep everything inside that had cracked and split open when John had called. She knew she couldn't. She hadn't even been able to wait a few minutes to calm herself before she called Ty.

"He'll get here," she told herself. "He'll help you figure out what to do." She paused at the window, though it didn't face the street and she wouldn't be able to see Ty when he arrived.

Her throat tightened at the thought of the holidays without Lexi and Hannah. At the thought of John marrying his secretary, of that woman being a stepmother to her daughters. She reminded herself that John was free to do what he wanted—that he always had done exactly that.

Brief bitterness brought a moment of fury to her mind, but she dismissed it as quickly as it had come. She had wasted months being angry, and she didn't want to do it again. Being angry at John had never made her any happier.

Helplessness filled her with every passing minute. Since Ty had brought up the idea of them getting married, since he'd said those absolute magical words—*I'm in love with you, River Lee*—in his cowboy drawl, River hadn't been able to stop thinking about him. About a future with him. About marrying him.

"How can I do that now?" she whispered, her words painful to her own ears. She'd already uprooted her daughters, taken them from the only grandparents they'd known and introduced them to a new grandma. She'd gone back to work, enrolled Lexi in a new school, and started dating someone new.

Dr. Thatcher had asked her what toll the girls had been paying at River's last appointment, only last week. River hadn't known how to answer. She'd been thinking about the doctor's question ever since, with no solutions coming to mind.

She seated herself at her desk and bowed her head, taking several long seconds to center her thoughts. *Lord,* she prayed. *What's the right thing to do for Lexi and Hannah?*

Since moving to Montana, her daughters had always been her focus. She constantly thought of them, and what would be best for them. They adored Ty, and she had never once thought his involvement in their life would hurt them.

And he had helped her so much. He loved her—and she loved him.

But could she marry him?

Now, when John was also getting remarried?

Ty will understand, she told herself. She opened her eyes and took a deep breath, but she still couldn't quite make her nerves or her pulse settle.

That didn't happened until Ty swept into her office, his arms strong and his cologne the scent of fresh air and grease. She didn't care. She let him gather her into his chest and whisper comforting things to her.

"Let's go to lunch," he said. "You haven't eaten, have you?"

She shook her head and left her office without her purse, a fact she didn't realize until she stepped up to the cash register at the Chinese register.

"It's fine," Ty said, pulling out his wallet. He ordered for her, and then himself, and guided River by the elbow to get her soda. She sat in the booth he put her in, the numbness surrounding her keeping the other conversations around her mute.

Ty sat down across from her, a tray of food in front of him. He nudged the container of orange chicken toward her and made a joke she didn't quite hear.

Her thoughts seemed so loud. Deafening almost. She

forked a piece of chicken but didn't put it in her mouth. She set the food and the fork back down. "Ty." She leaned across the table, a sense of clarity cutting through her jumbled mind.

"Yeah?" He mixed his chicken and rice together with quick little movements of his fork.

"Ty." She reached across the table and put both of her hands on his.

He looked up and went still. His beautiful eyes bored straight into hers.

"Ty, I love you."

A smile bloomed on his mouth, painting happiness into his eyes, into every line of his face. Pure joy. River didn't like the twist in her stomach, didn't like that her next words would take that smile down a notch. At least then it would only rival the starlight.

His fingers intertwined with hers. "I love you too, River Lee."

"I—I love you," she said again. "But I think we should…I don't know, slow things down a little bit." She searched his face as the smile faded. "For the sake of the girls."

"Slow things down?" he asked. "I see you for a total of six or seven hours on the weekends." He leaned back into the booth, his hands going with him. "I don't see how we can go much slower than that."

"I know." River sniffed, tired of crying.

Ty studied her, and she wilted under the weight of his scrutiny. Her fingers shook as she picked up her fork, but she could not put anything in her mouth.

"The girls will already be in turmoil over John's wedding."

Ty nodded, just once. Said, "So you're going to send them to Las Vegas?"

River nodded. "Yes," she whispered, the tears pressing against the back of her eyes. "I have to. They're his kids too, and he deserves to have them there for his wedding."

He reached for his soda and took a long drag. "I think that's probably the right decision." He leaned his elbows on the table and his eyes seemed to darken. "But I don't see how his wedding has anything to do with us."

"Lexi will miss a lot of school, and I don't know how they'll be feeling when they get back...." She let her voice pause there, not quite sure what else to add.

"We're not even engaged yet."

The way he said *yet* made her blood heat, and the mere thought of marrying him sent so much happiness through her that River felt lightheaded.

She let her hair fall over her shoulders as she nodded. "I know. And I don't think we can be for a while."

"How long?"

She shrugged, unable to look at him. "I don't know."

Several heartbeats of silence passed. Then several more. Then Ty said, "River Lee, does this really have to do with Lexi and Hannah?"

She pulled her gaze to his, a bolt of terror shooting straight to her heart. "I—"

"Because I don't think it does. They like me just fine, don't they?"

"Of course they do."

"We wouldn't get married until late spring or summer, at least, even if we got engaged right now. Are you saying we have to wait longer than that?"

A tear splashed her cheek, and she wiped it away. "I don't know."

He exhaled, a storm of emotion flowing across his features, discoloring those eyes she loved so much.

"You wanna know what I think?"

River did, but at the same time, she really did not. She nodded anyway.

Ty leaned forward again. "I think you're using your girls as a shield."

Whatever she'd thought he'd say, that wasn't it. "That's not true."

"Anytime you don't want to do something, you use them as a reason." His voice stayed quiet, but it possessed an anger she'd never seen from him before. "I know they need to come first for you. I understand that. I do. But I don't want to be third in line every time there's a major decision to be made. I realize that makes me selfish. Ridiculous even." He inhaled deliberately and the softness returned to his eyes.

"I love you, River Lee Whitely. I'm willing to be third behind Lexi and Hannah for real issues. But this." He waved his hand in the space between them. "This isn't about them and what's best for them at all. This is all about you."

CHAPTER 20

"Come on. I'll take you back to work." Ty got up, abandoning the food. He didn't look back as he walked out.

River sat at the table, dumbfounded. After only one breath, she launched herself into gear, her heels clicking on the tile as she followed him. A crisp autumn breeze pulled on her hair and jacket as she burst onto the street. "Ty!"

He turned, his hands stuffed down into his pockets, complete agony on his face.

She strode toward him, the storm inside her as tumultuous as what she sensed in him. "I'm tired of feeling numb," she said.

"I don't know what to say to that." He turned and kept walking.

"So that's it?" She caught up to him. "Are you breaking up with me?"

He pulled open her door, but she didn't get in. She stared him straight in the face. "Because I can't tell you when we can get married?"

"This doesn't have anything to do with me, either," he said. "But yeah, I think maybe we need a few weeks off so you can figure things out."

Her chin quivered though she was trying to be strong. "Ty—"

"Get in, River Lee. Please." He ducked his head, concealing his eyes with his cowboy hat. "I need to get back to the ranch."

———

A week later, River left her office at lunchtime again. This time it wasn't because her boyfriend had rushed to her aid. It was because she had an appointment with Dr. Fletcher. She'd been in once already that week, but she needed someone safe to talk to.

Her mother had been supportive of the decision to send the girls to Vegas for the holidays. River had called John and made all the arrangements. He'd fly to Butte, where she'd meet him at the airport, as she could not put her three-and-five-year-old on a plane by themselves.

River had sat by herself at church. She didn't even see Ty at the service, and she hated that he didn't show up. Didn't show up because of her.

But she'd felt calm about her decision to send the girls to

live with John for several weeks. While she hated everything about him getting married again, about her daughters having a stepmother, she'd come to terms with the fact that she couldn't control John's life. She could be there for her daughters—as Dr. Fletcher had told her on Monday. She could help them through anything they needed, be there when they asked questions or needed to talk. But she could not control everything about their lives.

River had spent her last session detailing everything about John's wedding and the girls that she never even made it to her relationship with Ty. His words had been floating around in her mind like ghosts, haunting her.

This is about you, River Lee. She even had the cowboy drawl down in her memory.

Never mind that he'd admitted to being selfish, jealous, and ridiculous. He'd never said anything about feeling that way. Never had she suspected that he felt that way. He never showed anything but adoration for Lexi and Hannah. Never demonstrated anything but joy to see River.

She didn't understand how she couldn't have known how he felt.

"River? Are you ready?"

River pulled herself from her thoughts as she looked up to find Dr. Fletcher standing in the doorway that led to her office. She flashed the only kind of smile she could, which meant her lips barely curved at all, gathered her purse, and went to spill her guts about Ty.

Dr. Fletcher handed River a can of diet cola before she sat down. "Good to see you again, River."

That was code for, "Why are you here again so soon?" River popped the top on her soda and took a long drink, letting the carbonation burn its way down her throat.

"I wanted to talk about Ty Barker," River said. "We broke up last week." Her voice stuck in her throat, and River lifted the soda to her lips again to try to clear the block.

Dr. Fletcher's eyebrows lifted, but she made no move to make notes. River appreciated the fact that Dr. Fletcher never typed during the conversation. Never wrote anything down. She participated in the conversation as if she were friends with her patients. River liked her far more than the man she'd seen in Las Vegas.

"Tell me what happened," Dr. Fletcher said.

"He came down after I called him, distressed about John's request for the girls—and his wedding. We went to lunch."

"Sounds nice."

"He broke up with me after I told him that we couldn't get married." River couldn't even look at the psychiatrist as she spoke. When she put it that way, it was no surprise that Ty had broken up with her. Why should he stay with her? Continue to drive down that treacherous canyon just to hold her hand during church, just to kiss her for a while after they ate lunch together?

And for what? To be constantly strung along until River said they could finally get married?

Her chest felt so cold. So cold. "I really blew it, didn't I?"

"It's normal to be cautious when considering a second marriage, especially when there are children involved."

River studied her hands. "Lexi and Hannah adore Ty. He's always bringing them treats from his mother's and little toys from the gas station." One more breath and she thought sure her lungs would crack. She took it anyway, and somehow, her organs kept working. "He played with them in the backyard, took them to the duck pond, all of it. He seemed smitten by them too."

"And how does he feel about you?"

"He—" River glanced up. "He told me he loved me a few weeks ago. We talked briefly about marriage. He said he'd wait as long as I needed." River took another drink, gulping until the can was empty. "At the time, I was thinking we could get engaged by Christmas and married by summertime."

"And why can't that still work?"

"I'm worried the girls—" River's words went mute and she struggled for breath. "I don't know how Lexi and Hannah will react to John's marriage. I thought me and Ty should wait."

"And he didn't want to wait?"

"He didn't think the problem was with the girls." River could barely hear her own words.

Dr. Fletcher leaned forward. "I'm sorry. Could you repeat that?"

River lifted her chin. "He didn't think the problem was with the girls." She cleared her throat but refused to look away from her doctor.

Dr. Fletcher didn't flinch. Didn't react beyond cocking

her head slightly to the side, her dark curls bouncing a bit as she did. "And what do you think is the problem?"

River's shoulders had never felt so heavy. She could only lift them halfway before they fell again. "That's why I'm here."

"I can't tell you what the problem is. Only you can figure that out."

"How do I do that?"

"What have you done in the past to figure things out? What did you do to know that it was right to leave Las Vegas? To move up here? To send the girls home for the holidays?"

"I thought about it. Prayed. Did what I felt like was right."

"So you do that here too."

"What if I already have and nothing feels right?"

"Being with Ty doesn't feel right?"

River shook her head. "I want to be with him. I love him."

"So is the problem with Ty?" Dr. Fletcher asked. "If it's not with you—if you love him as you claim to—and you think he's good for the girls—maybe the problem is with Ty. Has he said anything?"

"He indicated he'd felt jealous of the girls, like I put them first and he came third."

"That's a normal way for a man to feel. Even married men feel that way about their biological children sometimes."

River couldn't keep her fingers from twining together. Around and around they went. "He thinks I use the girls as reasons for things *I* don't want to do."

"Do you?"

"Maybe once or twice. But not with him."

"Well, he must've gotten that idea from somewhere."

River nodded. "I'll think about it."

Dr. Fletcher exhaled and stood. "While you're thinking about that, put yourself in Ty's boots. He's never settled down with anyone. Never dated anyone for longer than a few weeks. And then you find someone you like a whole lot. Someone you love. Someone you want to marry. And that person then says you have to wait for an unknown amount of time before that can happen. How might you feel? How might you react if the situation were reversed?"

River indicated she'd think about it with a quick nod. Then she got out of the office as quickly as she could, wishing, hoping, praying an answer would come so she didn't lose Ty forever.

"And one more thing to think about," Dr. Fletcher said when River's hand curled around the doorknob. "Why don't you want to marry Ty Barker?"

River spun back to the doctor. "I do want to marry him."

"Think about it." Dr. Fletcher turned away, the conversation clearly over.

———

Ty ducked his head and flipped up his collar as he stepped out of his cabin and faced the brutal early winter wind. It blew through his soul, the melancholy sound of it only adding to his depression.

Still, he faced the day the same way he had for the better part of a month: alone. Determined and alone. Only five more weeks until Jace took ownership of the ranch and Ty started as the foreman full-time. Maybe then he'd be busy enough to drive the echoes of River Lee from his mind.

That'll never happen, he thought as his footsteps trod on the frosted group. Fog hung in the air, and he hated it. Hated not seeing the sun in the winter. It had never bothered him as much as it did this year, and he once again wondered how he was going to make it through this winter alone.

He'd seen River Lee a couple of times at church. The other weeks he hadn't gone. Couldn't stomach making the drive and then not being able to hold her hand, share lunch with her, and kiss her goodbye.

Being in the same room with her and not being with her was the worst kind of torture he could imagine. So he'd decided to spend this Sunday morning with the horses. Anything would be better than seeing her white-blonde hair in those curls or in a high ponytail. He wasn't sure when her girls were leaving town, but it didn't matter now. She didn't need him. Her complete lack of communication over the past five weeks had proven that.

He brushed down two horses, fed the lot of them, and saddled Abra for a ride. He wouldn't be able to take the animal far, or go up to the highlands that he liked, but just sitting in the saddle calmed him.

"Yup," he said to the horse and the animal moved. Moved past the barns, past the machinery building, past all the cowboy cabins, even Tom's way down on the end away from the others. The trees had lost their leaves weeks ago, and it had already snowed several times. There was enough traffic in certain spots that the frozen ground showed through, and Ty took his horse along the well-worn path until it ended. He stopped and faced north, wishing he could just keep going.

Would anyone miss him? How long would it take for them to notice he was gone? Last time he'd gone out in the winter to fix the fence line and the vehicle had broken down, it had taken hours for anyone to know they hadn't come back in.

With today being a Sunday and a skeleton crew doing chores, Ty suspected he could disappear for the entire day and no one would know. He could possibly go off-grid until tomorrow morning before Jace would know.

Part of him really wanted to disappear. Leave Montana completely—and he'd never felt like that before. A slip of unease made his stomach sour. He'd never understood why his sisters had wanted to leave Gold Valley. Why River Lee had. And he absolutely hated that now he was gaining a bit of understanding in that area.

He shook the negative thoughts from his head and returned to the ranch. He wasted the day inside the warm walls of his cabin and suffered through a few more days until Thanksgiving. He helped with the morning chores, climbed in his truck, and headed down to his parents' house. He pulled up to the curb and parked behind his sister's rental car in the driveway.

"Should've taken some headache medicine," he muttered to himself. Just the thought of telling Vienna about River Lee made stabbing pains shoot behind his eyes. Eventually, it got too cold to sit in the truck without the heater blowing.

Ty went into the house and was met with laughter from his niece and nephew. The scent of roasting turkey and baking bread met his nose, and Ty relaxed.

"There you are." Vienna appeared in the mouth of the hall, her eyes bright and welcoming. "Get on over here."

Ty stepped into his sister's hug and then swept his four-year-old niece into a swooping embrace as well.

"Just you today?" Vienna eyed the doorway behind Ty like someone else would step through it.

"Just me." Ty set JJ on her feet.

"Mom said you'd probably bring your girlfriend."

"Nice try." Ty growled as he moved to enter the kitchen. "Mom knows I broke up with her."

"Why—?"

"I don't want to talk about it."

"Well, that's new."

He spun back to his sister. "What does that mean?"

"It means, little brother, that you've never had a problem telling me about your women friends. You always just laugh them off. This one must mean something."

Vienna might as well have stabbed him right through the

heart and then twisted the blade. Something must have shown on his face, because Vienna said, "Oh, honey. You loved her."

"Love," Ty said, arching one eyebrow. "Present tense. I'm nowhere near over her."

"You don't need to get over her."

Ty definitely thought he did. He couldn't keep living like this. Of course, his heart just kept beating, his lungs kept expanding, his brain kept thinking. So maybe he could live exactly like this.

"Maybe there's still hope for you two," Vienna said.

"River Lee is stubborn," Ty said.

"So are you," his sister said. "And River Lee Whitely? That girl you liked in high school?"

Ty sighed, the sound like a hissing snake. "The one and the same." He glanced to where his mom stood at the stove, stirring something, obviously listening. "Can we not talk about her today? Please?" He clapped his hands together in mock joviality and joined his mom in the kitchen. "I just want to eat turkey and mashed potatoes and some of your famous pecan pie."

His mom smiled and hipped him away from her with the admonition of "No tasting until lunchtime."

Ty chuckled, the first time he'd felt anything but glum since that fateful day when River Lee had called him. "All right."

He glanced at Vienna, who quickly put a smile on her face. But Ty wasn't fooled. He'd seen the serious look in her eye, the concern around the edges, and he knew he wouldn't escape this house before having at least one more conversation about River Lee with his sister.

He hadn't been able to articulate much more than "We broke up," to Jace and Caleb, but somehow he knew that with Vienna she wouldn't accept only three words for an explanation.

CHAPTER 21

*T*y leaned his head back and sighed. "Are we almost done?"

Vienna had been at it for almost forty-five minutes. The relentless questions. The way she could probe with only a look, a couple of well-placed words. Her children had no chance of surviving their teen years without Vienna knowing every single thing they did.

"Almost." Vienna took a sip of her tea, and Ty employed every ounce of his patience. He wasn't driving back up to the ranch tonight, and his mother hadn't gotten out the pie yet. She'd made herself scarce, and Ty was sure Vienna had somehow communicated to their mother that she needed some private time with Ty to get him to spill his guts.

And he'd complied. Answered every question from "Are you in love with her?" to "How much time did she say she needed?"

He liked the short answers. "Yes," to "Are you in love

with her?" and "She didn't know," to "How much time did she say she needed?"

Vienna had huffed at that one, which summed up Ty's feelings almost exactly.

"Ty, do you think, I mean, I'm a mother, so I understand her position. But do you think you could be happy even if you came third sometimes?"

Ty opened his eyes, wishing he'd disappeared downstairs with his father to watch football. "Yes," he said, looking straight at Vienna. "Yes, I'd be happy. I just need…. She's not ready."

"Why do you think that is?"

"I have no idea, Vienna. She sees a therapist. She'll figure it out."

"Wouldn't you rather be with her while she does than miserable by yourself?"

"Yeah, sure. But—"

His sister waited for him to go on, but Ty didn't know what to fill the silence with. Why shouldn't he be with River Lee while she figured things out? He could keep kissing her, holding her hand, talking with her.

"I need to go," he blurted, lurching forward on the couch.

Vienna placed her palm on his chest and pushed him back. Though he was twice as big as her, he stayed put. Something about the fiery look in her eyes kept him in place. She cocked her head. "Go where?"

"River Lee's."

She shook her head, the first indication of smile playing with her lips. "Give yourself a few days."

Ty moaned, sure he'd know why he couldn't jet over to River Lee's and profess his stupidity for leaving her. He might not even understand if he asked Vienna point-blank. He did anyway.

"Because, dear brother, you're desperate. And desperate doesn't look good on a man."

"Even if I show up with pecan pie and an apology?"

"Why do you think she hasn't called you yet?"

"I honestly have no idea, V. Just tell me."

"Because she wants to be whole when she talks to you again. She won't want to cry in front of you again. Give her a little more time—and definitely a warning before you show up on her doorstep."

"How much more time?" He hated that here he was again, asking how long he had to wait to be with River Lee.

"I don't know, Ty. You'll know when the time is right." Vienna got up, exhaled like her work here was done, and disappeared into the kitchen with the words, "I'll get the pie out," tossed over her shoulder.

Ty let Friday go by. And Saturday. Sunday morning, he rose early and got the morning chores done so he could go to church. He normally rode with Caleb and Holly, but today, he fired up his own truck and drove down the canyon. He'd left way too early, so he pulled over into the parking lot at the waterfalls.

His was the only truck, and he didn't dare get out for

fear of freezing to death. The edges of the river had frozen, but the fast-moving water of the falls were still liquid. He cracked the window enough to hear the roar of the water, let it wash over him, calm him from the inside out.

He hadn't called River Lee, and his nerves frayed a little more. He wasn't sure if he trusted himself to sit alone when River Lee had an empty spot next to her. Before, when he'd gone to church, he'd sat with Caleb and hadn't allowed himself to even look in River Lee's direction.

He took a deep breath of the river-scented air, rolled up his window, and turned his truck around. Only three cars sat in the parking lot at the church, so Ty stayed in his truck. As the minutes passed, more churchgoers arrived, until Ty felt like he could go in and not draw attention to himself.

He hadn't seen River Lee yet, and he wondered how she'd fared on Thanksgiving without Lexi and Hannah. His heart ached for her. "You should've been there," he chastised himself as he entered the church.

He paused in the doorway of the chapel, searching for that platinum blonde hair of River Lee's. He didn't find it, but he knew if she came, she'd sit in the middle of the chapel just like she always did. He sidestepped to the left side of the aisle, about two-thirds of the way back. That way, when River Lee arrived, he'd be able to see her.

Feeling stalkerish and desperate, he slid all the way to the wall, leaving the rest of the bench open for someone else. Vienna said desperation didn't look good on a man, but

Ty couldn't help it. He could only hope River Lee wouldn't see him when she came in.

She arrived five minutes later, and not only did she see him, she stared straight at him. Those aqua eyes pierced him, made his heart pound in such a way he thought it would burst from his chest.

He lifted his hand to acknowledge her and her step faltered. She yanked her gaze forward, steadied herself, and sat in her appointed row. She didn't look back at him. Didn't fidget. Didn't bow her head when it was time to pray.

But Ty did. He poured his whole soul out to the Lord, begging for the words to say to River Lee, the courage to talk to her, the ability to make things right between them.

Dr. Pinnion spoke about love. Such a simple subject, but upon further examination, it became more complex. Ty didn't understand how love worked, how it infiltrated the heart, how it hurt so much and yet brought so much joy.

The pastor wasn't speaking about romantic love, but everything he said resonated with Ty anyway. "When we love someone, we'll serve them," he said. "So if you're looking for the opportunity to get closer to the Lord and closer to someone in your life, service is the answer."

Service. Ty allowed his gaze to settle on River Lee. He could definitely figure out a way to serve her.

River hadn't been back to her house since she'd sent the

girls to Las Vegas. She couldn't stand to be in the house they'd bought to build their family without their laughter.

She'd been sleeping four or five hours a night, her mind consumed with Dr. Fletcher's questions. She'd realized her demands on Ty were bordering on ridiculous. She had reversed the situation, and she wouldn't want to be in a relationship that had no end in sight, no goal to be reached. She couldn't blame him for the way he'd acted. After all, she would've done the same to protect herself.

It was Dr. Fletcher's last request that needled at her. Over the several weeks, as she went to work, as she interviewed girls, as she packed up her daughters and sent them to their father's, she couldn't figure out why she didn't want to marry Ty.

But Dr. Fletcher had been absolutely right. The problem wasn't with Ty—it was with River.

She felt like she was dancing around what the real issue was, but she hadn't been able to uncover it yet. She'd gone to church every week, listened to every word the pastor said, prayed every time she felt hopeless—which was a lot.

So she went through the motions. She ate breakfast at her mother's table, the way she did as a child. She went to work and put in her time, the way she did as a teen. Without the girls, without Ty, she felt like she'd gone back in time thirteen years. She disliked her life now as much as she had then.

"Mom?" she asked one night after work.

"Mm?" Her mom sat at the kitchen counter while River stood at the stove, stirring a pot of soup.

"What happened to my father?" River had never heard her mother talk about her father. There were no pictures of him anywhere in the house. Growing up, River had never thought it odd—it was always just her and her mom. No dad needed.

Her mom didn't answer, triggering River to turn around. Her mom stared at her, pure panic on her face.

"Were you guys married?"

"Why—why does it matter?"

River leaned against the counter and couldn't look away from her mother. "It matters to me, because I think...well, I don't quite know what to think. I know I'm terrified of getting married again, but I think that's because of what happened with John." She sighed and glanced around the life her mother had built.

"I look around, and I don't see a man here. You're just fine without one. I was okay without a dad, but I want my girls to have someone—and not someone a thousand miles away in another city, with another wife."

River didn't quite know what she was saying, couldn't find the heart of her feelings, the reason for her questions. So she just kept talking. "I think I might be afraid to let Ty all the way in, because then I'd have to admit I want a man in my life." She met her mother's eye. "And you never needed that, and maybe that makes me weaker than you."

Her mother stood, the barstool scraping against the floor. "No, River Lee. You're not weak." She stepped into the kitchen and took River's shoulders in her hand. "I wasn't married to your father. I got pregnant really young—only seventeen—and he didn't want to marry me."

Tears formed in her eyes, but they stayed steady and strong. "So I determined I would raise you myself, that I could be both mom and dad. I did okay."

"You did great."

"But it doesn't mean it wasn't hard, or that you should do what I did."

The thought of raising Lexi and Hannah by herself sent fear through River. They needed a father figure in their life —and she wanted it to be Ty.

All at once, River understood her hesitation to open the door all the way for Ty to walk through. She'd never had a good example of a father figure in her own life. No dad in the home. And John had provided only monetarily.

She wanted mental support, emotional support, spiritual support. She just didn't know what it looked like, or how to take it.

She covered her mouth with her hand as the tears came. "How do I tell Ty?" she whispered.

Her mom gathered her into a hug. "Tell him what?"

"That I *need* him?"

Her mother cried with her, the words, "I don't know, River Lee. I never could tell your father that, and everything might have been different if I'd been able to," echoing in her head long after she'd calmed down, eaten, and gone to bed.

CHAPTER 22

*R*iver sat in the armchair that looked out her mother's front window, the snow falling on the other side of the glass magical and depressing at the same time. At least Silver Creek had called all non-essential personnel and told them to stay home.

Not that River had anything to do at her mother's house. Nothing besides stare at the snow and wish Ty was coming to see her later, kiss her under the fat flakes as they drifted down. Unconsciously, she touched her fingertips to her lips, the ghost of his kiss still there, even after all these weeks.

She sighed and leaned her head against the headrest, snuggling deeper into her hoodie. Now that she knew the problem—and that she had more than one—she wasn't sure how to overcome it. And she couldn't get in to see Dr. Fletcher for another week.

She knew she could get over her fear of marrying again. She already wanted Ty in her life long-term, and she knew intellectually that he wasn't John. Wouldn't do what John had done.

She was less sure she could make herself confess to Ty that she needed him. Even in her marriage to John, she'd taken care of everything. He never lifted a finger to clean anything. He'd come home late at night and make scrambled eggs and leave the pan for her to scrub in the morning.

And she did it.

She did the laundry, the dishes, the shopping, the bill paying. She alone took care of the kids, and if she had something that conflicted with her domestic duties, she hadn't asked John for help.

A blip of bitterness spread through her. No wonder her life hadn't changed all that much when she'd found out about his infidelity. Sure, she worried about money more often, but not enough to cause her to get a job in Las Vegas. No, she hadn't done that until she'd decided to move to Montana, and in truth, John's child support and alimony was probably enough to pay for a house and the barest of their necessities.

And River wanted more than that, the same way her mother had. A keen sense of exhaustion settled on River just thinking about her mother's life. River had never given it much thought at all. She and her mother had been happy, had everything they needed, and River had never wondered about her father.

At least not while growing up. She'd had a brief moment of longing when she'd gotten married, as she hadn't had a father to walk her down the aisle. She still hadn't thought to ask her mother about it.

But the story had poured out last week, after River had admitted that she wanted a father for her girls. She wanted a husband for herself. An equal partner, something John never was.

River's mother had moved to Gold Valley with her parents the summer she was pregnant with River. She didn't know it at the time, but when she found out, she contacted River's father. Also a senior in high school, he wasn't willing to move from Wyoming to Montana and become a father.

Once River's mother had decided to have the baby and then finish school, her parents had helped as much as possible.

River didn't remember them at all; they'd passed away from carbon monoxide poisoning when she was only four years old. Her mother had spoken of them often as River grew up; River had seen lots of pictures, but when she strained for any memories of them, they simply weren't there.

By then, River's mother had graduated from high school, gotten a few years of training in the real estate market, and was able to support herself and River just fine. No man needed.

You're not your mother, River thought. *It's okay to want a companion that's able to have intelligent conversations.*

She flipped her phone over, flirting with the idea of calling Ty right now. Instead, she closed her eyes and offered another prayer to know which path to take. Which call to make. And in the end, she heaved herself out of the armchair and went to leaf through a cookbook, deciding which cookie to bake.

Days passed. Snow fell and fell and fell. Christmas lights winked through the fog that seemed perpetual in the valley. With only a handful of days until the holiday, River had finally checked everything off her to-do list.

She'd mailed her presents to the girls. John had confirmed that he'd received them. She'd found the perfect pair of gloves for her mother. She'd given chocolate oranges to all her co-workers. She'd arranged to go to lunch with Jodi, where she planned to present the pair of fuzzy socks she'd bought for her friend.

It had been eight weeks since she'd last spoken to Ty. She saw him every week on the left side of the chapel. He always arrived before her, and his gaze seemed drawn to her when she walked in. He'd waved that first time, but since then, he simply stared for a few seconds. A few long seconds that made River's breath catch and her legs turn to lead. Then he dropped his gaze and hid his beautiful eyes beneath his cowboy hat.

She pulled into her mother's driveway, relieved she didn't have to go to work for a few days. The girls would be home in ten days, and as far as River was concerned, they couldn't pass fast enough.

River stepped from the car at the same time a truck pulled up to the curb behind her. Her heart spit out an extra beat and she turned to hurry into the house.

She reminded herself she wasn't in Vegas anymore, and

the person who had just pulled up was probably her mom's boyfriend. She turned back to welcome Milton and came face to face with Ty.

Her heart stopped completely now.

Wearing jeans, a black leather jacket, and that delicious cowboy hat, River had no defense against him. She told herself she didn't want a barrier between them and took a step in his direction.

"Hey," she said, thankful her voice didn't break or pitch toward the heavens.

———

Ty stood at the end of the driveway, his hands way down deep in his pockets. He'd pulled his cowboy hat down low and he watched River Lee as she continued taking slow steps toward him. He wanted to run to her, sweep her off her feet, and kiss her so completely she'd forget why she couldn't be with him.

She wore a pair of black slacks, heeled boots, and a blue coat that fell below her waist. He drank her in like a man who'd been in the desert for far too long. That white-blonde hair. The cold made her cheeks pinker than normal, accentuating her pale skin. She was so beautiful to Ty, and he fisted his hands to remind himself of his sister's rules for this encounter.

No kissing, he told himself firmly. In fact, he wasn't even going to get close enough to River Lee to touch her, though he wanted to very badly.

When she stood only ten feet away, he said, "I don't want to spend Christmas without you."

A smile enhanced her beauty and erased the ache that had been staining Ty's soul for the past two months.

"Maybe we can get together sometime in the next few days," he continued. "Dinner maybe?" He hoped his desperation didn't carry in his voice. It sounded somewhat normal to him, and he couldn't report back to Vienna that he'd begged. She'd expressly told him *not* to beg.

"I'd like that," River Lee said.

Ty flashed a grin but erased it quickly. Vienna had coached him not to act too happy if River Lee agreed. He had to hold his cards close to the vest for a little while. If he didn't, he wasn't sure his heart would ever recover.

She moved closer to him. Close enough for him to catch a whiff of her floral scent. He worked hard not to take a deep breath of her.

"I wanted to tell you something," he said. "But maybe you'd rather wait until we go out."

"Now's fine."

"It's mighty cold out here." He fell back two steps, his breath hanging in the air between them. "I'll talk to you on say, Friday? Dinner on Friday night?"

A frown passed through her bright-as-the-sea eyes before she smiled. "Sure, Friday's fine."

"Great. I'll come pick you up about seven. Is that okay?" He turned halfway back to his truck like he had something much more pressing to get to. He did. Breathing. He couldn't seem to get a proper lungful with River Lee so close, so close, so close.

So close and talking to him to boot.

"That's fine."

He nodded, noting she'd said fine three times now, and escaped back to the safety of his truck. He fired up the engine and took off at what he hoped was a normal, neighborhood speed. He turned the corner and forced himself to drive another half a block. Then he pulled over and called his sister.

"So?" she asked. "How did it go?"

Ty finally allowed the joy he'd been holding back to penetrate his façade. A grin split his face. "I think it went real well."

"You asked her out?"

"I suggested dinner on Friday. She agreed."

"So she talked to you? How did she seem?"

Ty leaned his temple against the window. "She seemed... okay."

"Okay?" Vienna's voice sharpened. "What does that mean?"

"She looked tired. Stretched thin. It's no wonder. Her kids have been gone for weeks, and it seems like she's living at her mom's again." Ty's mood darkened as he pictured River Lee. She had looked worn down, but that could've been because she'd had a long day at work. Not because she missed her girls—and him—with the fierceness of gravity.

"What did she say?" Vienna asked.

"She said fine a lot," Ty said. "I'm kinda worried about that."

"You showed up at her place unannounced. She talked to you; that's all that matters."

"It was her mom's place."

"That just makes you more out of place," Vienna said. "You have no reason to be in that neighborhood, so she knows you came specifically to talk to her."

"I did go specifically to talk to her."

"And she knows it."

Ty rubbed his forehead and reminded himself that he'd asked for Vienna's help. She'd made him wait three weeks, and every day, every hour, every breath had felt laced with poison. But he'd waited. And now he'd gotten a date with the woman he couldn't live without. His smile returned and even twenty more minutes of dissecting everything he'd said, where he'd kept his hands, what River Lee had looked like couldn't erase his grin.

Friday came, and Ty was suddenly made of all thumbs. He couldn't seem to get the chores done the right way. He dropped a screwdriver into an engine after breakfast, and lost the keys to the administration lodge about mid-morning.

His brain had completely abandoned him, putting him a foul mood. He located the keys and fished the tool out of the tractor before joining Caleb and Jace for lunch in the admin lodge. Miss Gloria, the matron of Horseshoe Home, had been making more food than even the cowboys could eat. She usually wept when she brought it over to the lodge, and Ty wasn't sure he had it in him today to watch her wrestle with her emotions. His were suffocating him already.

The transition of ownership had been emotional for everyone, Ty included. He'd be moving sometime in January, and taking on all the foreman responsibilities, and he didn't know if he could do nearly as well as Jace had done for the cowboys.

Gloria handed him a bowl of her famous beef stew, and Ty flashed her a grateful smile—right before he fumbled the bowl and dumped it all over himself. Some of it may have even splashed on Gloria.

"Oh, boy." Jace stepped next to where Ty stood frozen, thick broth dripping down his jeans. "Someone's havin' a rough day."

Ty thawed and accepted the napkins Gloria held toward him. He mopped himself up as best as he could, accepted another bowl of stew, and hurried back to his own cabin. Dinner couldn't come fast enough.

CHAPTER 23

 y stopped at the waterfalls, suddenly second-guessing everything about himself. Were his jeans dark enough? Should he have worn his coat instead of the leather jacket? If this was the right thing to do, why was his gut turning over and over and over?

Vienna had texted just as he was leaving the ranch. Her *Good luck! Call me when you get home* message had meant the world to him.

He sent a message to River Lee: *Where should I pick you up? Are you staying at your mom's?*

Yes, my mom's came back in only a few seconds.

When Ty arrived, River Lee opened the front door and glided down the front steps. Ty leapt from the truck and met her on the sidewalk. Vienna had given him specific instructions for this date too—no kissing until the drop-off. Ty wasn't sure he could wait that long.

"Hey, River Lee," he said, unsure of the line between

them. It felt like they'd just met for the first time, and there was definitely a boundary between them he didn't want to cross.

She beamed at him. "Where are we going?"

"I thought we'd go to the steakhouse. Is that okay?"

River Lee paused and peered up at him, an intensity in her eyes he missed. "Are you going to ask me all night if everything is okay?"

"No, ma'am," he said automatically.

She swatted his chest, and Ty took her playfulness as a good sign. "Do not call me ma'am." She linked her arm through his and towed him with her around the truck. "I like the steakhouse just fine."

Ty opened her door for her but held onto her. "Are you going to use the word fine a lot tonight?"

She blinked and then laughed. "I hope not." She climbed into the truck and Ty went around to get in beside her.

He didn't back out of the driveway though. He gripped the steering wheel and said, "I don't really care about what happened when we broke up." He stared out the windshield at her mother's garage door. "It's all water under the bridge to me." He finally turned his head and trained his eyes on her. "I love you, and I want to make it work." He swallowed. "I didn't mess things up too badly, did I?"

River Lee's throat worked and Ty saw the determination enter her face. She slid across the seat, positioned herself right next to him, and slid her fingers up his arm. "You didn't mess anything up," she whispered. "That was me."

Ty shook his head. "I told you I'd wait forever. It's my fault for bein' jealous of your girls."

"No." Her touch on the back of his neck made him shiver, made River Lee smile despite the seriousness of their conversation. "You were right. I was hiding behind the girls." She met his eye. "I need you, Ty. I want you. I love you."

Ty was going to have to apologize to Vienna, because he was going to kiss River Lee before they even left the driveway.

And she let him. Kissed him back. Healed the hole that had been plaguing him for his entire life.

———

River kissed Ty like her life depended on having her lips on his. By the time he broke their connection with a husky chuckle, the window behind him had fogged slightly. She snuggled into his side as he reset his cowboy hat and put the truck in reverse. She waited until they'd arrived at the steakhouse and been seated before she started her explanation. Ty listened to her childhood story about her absent father and how she'd been afraid to admit she wanted and needed a man in her life.

"And am I that man?" he asked, his food almost gone he'd been silent so long.

River Lee had hardly touched her fillet mignon and baked potato. She cut off a small piece of her steak and popped it into her mouth. "I guess you'll have to wait and see."

He growled, which caused River to laugh with delight. She leaned her elbows on the table, beyond happy to be here with him. Everything about it felt right, and she pressed her eyes closed in a long blink of bliss.

*R*iver paced in her office as she waited for Ty. Last time she'd been this nervous, Ty had broken up with her.

"That's not gonna happen today," she muttered to herself. She'd asked him to come down to the valley and take her to lunch. Though it was near the end of March, winter was hanging on. It had foiled her plan for the past several days, but when this morning had dawned bright and clear, she'd called Ty immediately.

He'd agreed to pick her up at her office, and she had the front secretary on alert to his arrival.

He should be here any—

"Ty has arrived." Shelly's voice came over River's speaker in a hushed whisper. "He is so handsome," she added, which made River grin.

She wiped the smile from her face when her door

opened and Ty appeared with all his handsomeness in tow. "You ready?"

"No," she said. "Come in for a minute."

Ty obliged and collapsed into the chair where her girls usually sat.

"How's life as the foreman?" she asked.

A grin the size of Texas graced his face, lighting River's entire universe. "It's great. I love it. It's just busy."

She sat down in the chair next to him, her chest tight with the words she needed to say. "Ty." She cleared her throat.

He looked at her and reached for her hand. "Yeah?"

"I think we should get married."

Ty blinked at her, his dark eyes sharp and serious.

"At the Harvest Festival," River added. Was this how men felt when they proposed? She didn't like the disquiet, the absolute horror that he might say no.

"You want to get married in August?" he asked.

"Yes." She studied him, trying to find the root of his disbelief. "It's only five months, but I think I can put together a wedding that fast."

"Putting the wedding together is the least of my concerns," he mumbled.

"What are your concerns?"

"Well, to start with, we haven't talked about where we'll live or anything," he said. "And did you forget how I told you last week that I was terrified of being a good dad?"

River's heart stuttered. "Are you saying no?"

Ty kicked a grin in her direction. "Of course not." He

dropped to his knees in front of her and took both her hands in his. "River Lee, will you marry me?"

"I just asked you that."

"I didn't hear you ask me anything." He grinned for all he was worth. "I heard you say you wanted to get married during the Harvest Festival. There wasn't even a question in there."

She shook her head, her own smile lifting her lips. "You're a cheater. But I love you anyway."

"*I* love *you*." He touched his lips to hers, barely hanging on for a breath before deepening the kiss. "I think I can be a decent dad," he murmured against her lips. "Do you think I can do a good job with the girls?" He moved his lips down her jaw to her neck.

"Of course," she said breathlessly. "You'll be a great dad."

He pulled back and took a deep breath. "All right. Let's get married during the Harvest Festival."

River squealed and threw her arms around Ty. "I'll put you first sometimes, cowboy."

"I'm not worried about it, River Lee."

She adored the way he drawled her name and she melted into his embrace. "Is there room in your big ol' foreman cabin for me and two little girls?"

He cupped her face in his capable hands. "You want to live on the ranch with me?"

She gave a half-shrug. "You mentioned once that the more I rode a horse, the more I'd like it. I thought living up on the ranch would give me the opportunity to figure out what's so magical about horseback riding."

He smiled and chuckled. "Just as long as you promise not to try to trample me."

She laughed too, and said, "I love you, Ty."

"I love you too." Ty kissed her one more time, ready to go horseback riding with her, spend every day with her, and be the best dad he knew how to be.

———

Read on for a sneak peek at **THE CHRISTMAS COWBOY COMPETITION**, the next book in the Horseshoe Home Ranch Romance series.

*A*rcher Bailey stepped out into the tiny backyard of his townhome and inhaled. Ah, yes. The crisp scent of freshly mowed grass mingled with the underlying scent of mountain water and a slightly chlorinated whiff from the pool a few hundred yards away.

Today was the day. Today, he was going to land the job that would start his career. Today was the day his life would change.

He lifted his hand to his black cowboy hat, the hint of fall already in the valley though Labor Day still lingered a week away. Sometimes Montana saw snow in September, and Archer loved it. Loved everything about Gold Valley, and horses, and hopefully, Horseshoe Home Ranch, where he had an interview in three short hours.

Then his father could stop riding him for quitting college. For giving up a scholarship Archer had earned by the skin of his teeth and pure luck. For coming home without a job or a direction he wanted to go in.

His little buckskin-colored dog sniffed around his feet as the sliding glass door just across the fence opened. Carrot Cake immediately started barking, easing when the gorgeous blonde removed her hat and crouched, extending the tips of her fingers through the slats in the fence to give Carrot a scrap of cheese.

"You know he's on a diet," Archer said, trying not to rake his gaze up and down Emersyn Ender's body. They'd lived next door to each other for two years. Shared a wall, a fence, and his dog for twenty-four long months.

At first, Archer had thought they could make a go of a relationship. But Emery radiated a coldness he'd never experienced, not even in the depths of a Montana January. She held everything close to the vest, rarely said more than five words to him, and kept mostly to herself.

"He looks like he's lost some weight."

"Hmph." Archer sipped his coffee, sure Carrot Cake had only lost a few ounces and only because of the grooming Archer had done on him late last week.

"How's the job hunt going?" She tucked her hands into the back pockets of her shorts and looked beyond him, over the waist-high fence that separated their private yards from the common areas of the complex. She always did this sort of looking past him thing, like he was some foul ogre she couldn't bear to look directly at.

He shifted his feet self-consciously, wanting to keep his

job interview a secret. After all, Emery had stolen his last opportunity right out from under him.

That's not fair, he thought immediately, but the familiar disappointment and his old friend bitterness pressed against the back of his tongue anyway.

"I have an interview today," he said, unsure of when his brain had told his vocal chords to speak.

Emery focused on him, her bright blue eyes startling and absolutely beautiful. Archer took another gulp of coffee. "That's great, Archie."

So she had a nickname for him. He hated it. Didn't mean they were friends.

"Where?" she asked.

"Oh, up at the ranch." Four ranches surrounded Gold Valley, and he kept it vague on purpose. "How are things at Silver Creek?"

They'd both gone out for the same job at the teen reha-bilitation center last spring. In the end, the director there decided he wanted a female equestrian trainer where he'd always, always had a male. She'd gotten the job. Archer had slunk home like a pup with its tail between his legs. He waited for her to take her garbage can out on Wednesdays so he didn't run into her. Then he brought both cans in at night to avoid her further. The lengths he'd gone to in order to save face had astounded even him.

Emery sighed, a long drawn-out hiss that raised an alarm in Archer's system. "It's fine. But my twelve-week program ends on Friday. Then I'm out of a job."

"Oh." Archer didn't know what else to say. His first inclination was to ask if her job would be available, but he didn't want to seem overeager or rude or unsympathetic. Truth was, he felt a kindred soul in Emery as she'd bounced from as many jobs as he had over the years. She didn't seem to have a parent rubbing her nose in it though.

"Good luck with your interview." Emery flashed him a smile that, if she'd allow it to reach her eyes and light up her whole face, would be a sight to behold. She tucked her hair behind her ear and went back inside her house, much to Carrot Cake's disconcertion.

"Oh, quiet down, you." Archer toed the whiny dog back into his own townhouse and shut out the world. Shut out Emery. Shut out everything. He needed to find his center if today was really going to be the day that started his life.

He dropped to a sitting position in the living room and crossed his legs. With his eyes closed, he prayed in a whisper, "Please help me say all the right things during the interview."

Please, please, please pretty much dominated the rest of his meditation session. By the time he left to get up to Horseshoe Home Ranch, Archer wasn't sure if any of his prayers or the minutes he spent meditating actually did anything but waste time.

———

Emery didn't waste a single moment after she left Archer standing in his backyard. He hadn't told her where the job was—purposefully, she knew—but she had a laptop and their community provided fantastic fiber Internet service as part of the HOA fees.

It only took her a single search and a quick scan of one job board to find the listing for a cowhand at Horseshoe Home Ranch. She worried the inside of her cheek with her teeth as she read the description. She'd grown up on a small farm in Wyoming until age twelve; she'd ridden horses since the age of five, and had begun training them when her father left them all behind. But she'd seen him tag cows, and fix fences, and move sprinkler pipes. How hard could it be?

And bonus, she knew Jace and Belle Lovell from church. Well, "knew" was probably a huge stretch, but at this point, Emery had to play every advantage she had. She needed a job, one that paid well enough to keep her in this townhome and allowed her to keep sending money to her sister in Spokane.

The twinges of guilt strumming through her body were easily covered by the desperate need to keep Glenna going. Her sister worked at a big box store, paid her own rent, and scraped by with cheap groceries bought with her employee discount. Emery paid all the utilities. The Adult Services group in Spokane provided her transportation, so that was a relief.

She jotted down the number for the ranch, stuffing the last moments of regret to the soles of her feet. It was a job. Heaven knew Archer wasn't the only candidate for it, and just because Emery wanted to throw her hat into the ring didn't mean he didn't have a good chance.

"Better than you," she mumbled to herself as she carefully punched in the numbers. The line rang and her stomach did flips. One, two, three. Finally a woman said, "Hello?"

"Yes, hello, I'm calling about the cowhand job. Is it still available?"

"Uh, let's see." Scratching came through the line, something like the shuffling of papers. "Yes, today's the last morning of interviews. Looks like we're booked, though. Let me see...." More scuffling and then a loud *bang!* hurt Emery's ears.

"Oh my stars." The woman's tinny voice sounded light years away. "I'm so sorry," she said normally now. "I dropped the phone. Can I give you a call back in a few minutes? I'll go talk to Jace and see if he can do one more interview, all right?"

"Sure, yeah, all right." Though she didn't want to end the call without a scheduled appointment—especially if today was the last day Jace was doing interviews—Emery didn't really see what other choice she had. She gave the woman her name and phone number and hung up.

She needed to be over at Silver Creek by two o'clock, but the woman had said "morning of interviews" so hopefully Emery could do both.

A high-pitched whirring sound came from the townhouse to her left—Archer's place. She'd never asked him what he did every morning to make that sound, but it lasted less than a minute, and Emery had assumed it was a high-end blender. *Probably a smoothie junkie,* she thought, adding an eyeroll to her mental musings.

Emery never ate breakfast and rarely consumed more than fruits, nuts, and vitamin water anyway. Her stomach didn't seem to play nicely with much more. She paced from her kitchen to her front door, which took about ten steps. Turn. Pace back.

She had more productive things to do around the house, like fold laundry and clean bathrooms, but she couldn't seem to make her mind settle on anything but the job at Horseshoe Home.

Eventually, she pulled out the disinfectant wipes and swept them over countertops, light switches, and walls, waiting for her phone to ring. She did all the dishes and had just moved into the half-bath to get the toilet sparkling when her device finally chirped.

She scrambled for it and breathlessly answered the unknown number. "Emery?" the woman asked. "It's Belle from Horseshoe Home. Jace says he's happy to have you come up this morning. Does eleven o'clock work for you?"

"Yes, absolutely, sure." Emery checked herself and took a big breath. "I'll be there."

"Great." Belle wore a smile in her voice. "The interview will be in his office, which is in the administration lodge. It's the second biggest house up here, on the right-hand side of the road."

"Sounds good." Emery hung up and pressed her eyes closed. Now she just needed to get this job so she could continue to help her sister maintain her lifestyle.

A few hours later, Emery seated herself in the run-down Jeep she used for a vehicle. The engine had almost two-hundred-fifty thousand miles on it, but it was still trucking along. Emery had named the Jeep Jenny at the first hundred thousand miles, and she prayed every morning and every night that her car would be spared any wear and tear, that it would keep running, and so far God had granted her that minor miracle.

She exited the community where she lived and turned right. The canyon and the glorious horseshoe shaped falls bloomed before her very eyes, and a quick rush of gratitude reminded her of how lucky she was to live in such a beautiful place.

The ranch only sat twenty minutes from her front door, and she arrived earlier than she'd anticipated. Butterflies the size of dinner plates crashed into her abdominal lining, and she thought sure she'd need to throw up before entering the appointed building.

With one final cramp and a deep breath, Emery left Jenny's safety and mounted the front steps. Through the doors, she came to a desk with a weathered cowboy sitting behind it.

"Mornin', ma'm," he said. "You here for the interviews?"

"Yes, sir."

"Chair right there." He pointed with the pen he held in his right hand toward an empty row of white folding chairs. At least she didn't have to see any of the other applicants. Her own cowgirl boots clicked against the tile as she made her way to the chairs and sat.

Eleven o'clock came and went. A few cowboys worked in the open area filled with desks. Laughter came from a doorway in the back that had bright fluorescent lights spilling from it. The scent of marinara and meat came from that direction too, and Emery's stomach grumbled. A hallway sat across from the kitchen and went left into areas she couldn't see.

Impatience gnawed at her thoughts, making her right toe tap, tap, tap against the tile. She had no idea how long this interview would take, and she still needed to grab lunch and get all the way across town to Silver Creek by two.

Finally, finally, after sitting there for a half an hour—and twenty of those minutes were past her appointed interview time—a pair of men appeared in the hallway. They paused, and Emery's focus razored in on them.

One—the slightly taller man—was Jace Lovell, owner. The other—with his signature black cowboy hat—was Archer Bailey, rival and neighbor.

Panic poured through Emery in waves. He would see her. There was no way he *wouldn't* see her. She needed to move now.

Now!

But her body remained as limp and lifeless as a sack of potatoes. Everything slowed around her except her pulse, which only seemed to be accelerating. Faster and faster while everything else blurred behind a layer of wax paper.

Jace smiled. The two of them shook hands. Archer turned toward her. He stepped, and stepped, Jace right behind him.

Why did it take so long for him to make it to the front of

the room? Why was Emery's chest so tight? Why did her fingers ache and pulse with their own heartbeat?

"Emery?" The level of surprise in Archer's voice shocked Emery out of the weird warpy thing that had just happened. "What are you doing here?"

She leapt to her feet, every cell in her body buzzing like someone had hooked her to a live wire and turned the electricity up high.

"She's my last interview," Jace said, joining them and extending his hand for Emery to shake. "C'mon back, Emery. Good to see you again, Archer." He turned and walked away, but Emery couldn't move.

Archer glared at her with more menace than she knew he possessed. He'd always been nice to her, probably nicer than he should've been given how little attention she'd given him over the years. He brought her garbage can in when it snowed heavily, and he'd fixed her fence when the gate slammed into it.

He could've said all kinds of things in this situation. Breathed threats at her. Delved into a long lecture about his disgust for her. All of it was plain to see right there in his deep, dark eyes. Eyes that had always sucked at Emery's resolve, always beckoned that if she just dove in, she'd like what happened after that.

He said nothing. Just marched past her and out the door.

SNEAK PEEK! THE CHRISTMAS COWBOY COMPETITION
CHAPTER TWO

$\mathcal{F}$ury boiled in Archer's gut, and he did not like it. No, he did not like it, not one little bit. Somehow he managed to navigate his toy-sized truck down the canyon without smashing into a cement barrier or going off the road and hitting a tree. A small miracle, really, given the level of annoyance altering his vision.

By the time he pulled into his driveway, the smell of hot rubber and the sharp metallic scent of his engine filled the cab. He really couldn't push his truck like that; it was barely hanging on to the last days of its life. And Archer had no way to pay to replace it or repair it. He would not be asking his father, who had talent under the hood of a vehicle.

Still, he practically gunned the engine once the garage door lifted, nearly crashed right into the deep freezer he had against the back wall, which held a box of corndogs and several cartons of pistachio ice cream.

He snatched the corndogs on his way inside and threw

them on the counter, startling Carrot Cake. The little dog whined, and Archer softened. "Sorry, bud. But you would not believe that woman." He spun to turn on the oven, nearly knocking over the high-powered blender that he used every morning for his protein shakes.

"I can't believe her. I—just—can't—believe—" He stopped talking, his frustration so foul he couldn't even form coherent words. He put three corndogs on a baking tray and slammed it into the still-warming-up oven. He made loud *cracks!* and *bangs!* as he got out the ketchup and mayo and mixed up a dipping sauce for his meager lunch.

His mother would caution him to put something green on the plate. "Or some grapes, Arch. *Something* from the plant family." Her voice rebounded through his head. At least she only lectured him about his dietary choices. His father lectured him about *all* of his choices, and Archer pulled an apple from the fridge and chomped into it while he waited for the rest of his food to cook.

The full twenty minutes for the corndogs to bake passed before Archer felt his fury fade. He didn't want to be home when Emery returned, so he packed everything onto a plate and went back out to his truck. He managed to leave his house and get down the street without seeing her. Thankfully. He couldn't predict what he'd do next time he came face-to-face with her.

Moments later, he pulled into the parking lot at the waterfalls and got out. With school starting last week, there were noticeably less families here, and he found a table easily. Desperation coated his tongue along with the grease from the corndogs. What would he do if he lost another job to Emery Ender?

His mind imploded at the very thought of it. He'd have to move. And not just across town. But out of state.

She'd never rubbed in the fact that she'd been hired at Silver Creek over him, but Archer's pride wouldn't allow him to live next door to her if she got this job and he didn't. No way. Couldn't happen.

He needed this job, and not only because it was a job that would pay the bills. He needed it to start his career. He needed it to show his father he wasn't going to bounce from temp job to temp job for the next twenty years. He needed it to boost his own confidence, which seemed to have fallen in the gutter last Christmas and made a permanent home there.

The interview had gone great. Archer had practically floated toward the front of the administration lodge—until his gaze had landed on Emery. Everything inside him had revved up and then shut down, almost within the same breath. He'd learned from his father that sometimes saying nothing was more hurtful than yelling, so he'd strode out without a backward glance.

"Better get a back-up plan, Arch," he told himself. He pulled out his phone and navigated to the online job boards for Gold Valley. He'd have better luck securing a more long-term job in a bigger city, but he loved the town where he'd grown up. His parents still lived in the four-bedroom blue house in Monkeytown, and both of his brothers had left for their careers, leaving him with the responsibility of looking after the house and his parents as everything aged.

Archer didn't mind. He didn't have a fancy computer science degree like Charlie; didn't design the biggest video games on the market while sipping skinny mocha lattes and wearing hippie sandals around Bellevue, Washington. Archer also didn't have a highfalutin engineering degree like Xan, who lived in Huntsville, Alabama and worked for NASA.

Seriously, *NASA*? How was Archer supposed to compete with that?

But compete his father expected. So when Archer had dropped out of college and moved into a townhome he could barely make the payment on, his father's disappointment carried on the wind from his house across town.

Archer had been looking for something he could do as a career and not have a degree for. He loved hiking, being outside with the fresh air and the scent of pines. He loved horses, and had thought for a couple of weeks there that he could make a career out of working with wayward boys and horses.

That hadn't worked out, but Archer had learned that he was supposed to be a cowboy. He just needed a ranch that was hiring. He'd checked the job boards every day for seventy-three days before a job came up at Horseshoe Home.

He got to his feet and tossed his trash in the nearby can. And that blasted Emery Ender had honed in on his job, had dared to call and get an interview that very morning. He shook his head, wanting to be angry, but his emotions had been spent.

Still unwilling to go home until he knew Emery would be at work, he went to McCall's, the gas station that used to mark the edge of town, back before all the new housing developments closer to the falls and the mouth of the canyon had been built.

"Afternoon, Arch," Myron said from his perch on the counter-high stool just inside the convenience store. He sat in the window and watched all the comings and goings of Gold Valley. Archer had never seen the man wear anything but jean overalls with either a blue, a yellow, or a white shirt underneath. And Myron always chewed a piece of peppermint gum. "Keeps my breath minty," he'd told Archer when he'd asked about it.

"Afternoon." Archer went over to the cooler and pulled out a sports drink. He paid and then sagged his weight against the counter, the indentation there from the countless people who'd come to the gas station for refills and refreshment and gotten it in more ways than one.

"What's eatin' you?"

"Nothing." Archer took a swing from his bottle.

"Right." Myron cocked one eyebrow at him, and Archer whipped off his hat to mimic the action.

Myron ducked his left and seemed to get his right all the way to his hairline. Archer smiled as he repeated the action. He wiggled one up and down while the other stayed still. Myron filled the convenience store with laughter and waved one hand. "You win."

"I always do." He sobered when he realized how untrue the words really were. "Can I ask you a question?"

"Sure."

"You've owned this station and store for a while, right?"

"Forty-seven years. My daddy owned it before that."

Archer actually envied that kind of stability. The idea that Myron knew what his life would be and had embraced it. "Exactly."

"Exactly what?"

"I applied for a job today," Archer said, not really sure where he was going with the conversation. "I really want it."

Myron simply waited, his eyes watching the gas pumps and his lips smacking as he chewed, chewed, chewed that gum.

"So if you had a job you really wanted, what would you do to get it?" Archer asked.

Myron took a long time to lift one of his beefy shoulders, today's yellow shirt bunching where his arm met his body. He wore a dark gray cowboy hat—the same one Archer had seen dozens of times before.

"Yeah, I don't know either," Archer said. He glanced around the old store, appreciating the vintage signs, the way the coolers kept on humming, the scent of nacho cheese and warming hot dogs on rollers.

"Oh, I know," Myron said just as the bell on the door chimed and a mother entered with her two preschool-age children.

Archer glanced at them but focused quickly back on Myron when he said, "I'd fight for it. Do everything I could to get it." He shrugged his other shoulder this time. "I mean, if it was what I wanted."

Nodding, Archer stepped out of the way so the woman could buy her gas and her children's suckers.

He couldn't make Jace give him the job. Archer would get a phone call with a decision. How was he supposed to fight that?

———

Emery was not expecting to see anyone sitting on her front porch when her headlights cut a swath of light across the front lawn she shared with Archer. She pulled all the way into her garage, her heart tip-tapping out an irregular beat.

She kept Jenny running and the doors locked while she waited for the garage door to come down. Only then did she dare turn off the car and go into her house. Seconds later, someone knocked.

A man, judging by the heavy fistfalls.

Emery knew who it was. And she knew Archer wouldn't go away. She'd really hoped to avoid this confrontation. She'd been relieved when she'd returned home from her interview to find his place silent, dormant. And at nine-thirty-five PM, after her shift at Silver Creek, she honestly hadn't expected he'd want to do this tonight.

"C'mon, Emery," he called through the door. "I know you're in there."

She deposited her purse and keys on the kitchen counter

and went to the door, yanking it open right when he was about to beat on it again.

He lowered his fist and then stuck it in his pocket. He wore jeans that hugged his thighs in all the right ways, that delicious cowboy hat, and a shirt the color of apricots. She wanted to laugh at him about the shirt, but he made the soft peachy color look sexy, and all she could do was lick her lips and wait for him to chew her out.

She deserved it. She shouldn't have looked up his job and applied for it. Regret had been lancing through her all afternoon, especially when Dr. Richards had given a lesson on integrity to all the girls right before their riding lesson. Apparently, he'd been having a problem with theft at Silver Creek, and he wanted the girls to know that integrity was about more than just being honest.

Before Archer could say anything, Emery said, "I'm sorry, Archie. I shouldn't have gone up there this morning."

He blinked at her, his strong jaw muscle twitching as his teeth ground together. She sighed and stepped back, a clear invitation for him to enter her house. He didn't, and she was glad he didn't. She'd never invited him inside before, and she didn't know why she'd thought now would be a good idea.

"I can't even do that job," she said. "Jace asked me about lifting a hay bale, and wrestling with a full-grown cow to give medication." She gave a mirthless laugh to go with this miserable day. "And there's no way I can set a fence post by myself. He said cowhands often do that kind of stuff." Sure, she had some experience from her childhood, but she simply wasn't as strong as a man.

Archer just stood there, and she wondered how long he'd been waiting on her porch, and why he wouldn't say something.

She finally asked, "What do you want?"

"Why do you need this job so badly?" he asked.

"I have bills to pay." She folded her arms across her chest, as if that would somehow keep the truth inside.

He shook his head slowly, everything about him a shadow from his raven hair, those dark diamond eyes, and his black cowboy hat. "There has to be more than that going on here."

"Why's that?" She cleared her throat when her voice strayed into an upper octave.

"You just admitted that you've applied for a job you can't do. Why don't you go, oh, I don't know. Waitress or work at the elementary school or be a checker at the grocery store?"

She settled her weight onto her back foot, the fight in her rearing to the front of her skull. "Oh, and leave the real work to the men, is that it?"

"No."

"You do realize there are male waiters, right? And teachers too, shockingly."

"Of course. I just meant—"

"I know what you meant."

"No, you don't," he argued. "I meant that—just—why apply for a job you can't do when there are tons you can?"

The dull ache behind her eyes she'd been fighting for

hours started to throb. She needed to eat and take some painkiller and get to bed. She couldn't stand here in her doorway for much longer, breathing in the woodsy quality of Archer's skin or the fresh waterfall scent of his clothes.

"I'm sorry," she said again. "I'll call up to the ranch in the morning and tell Belle I can't do it, that they shouldn't consider me."

"They?" Archer asked.

"Yeah, Belle came into my interview too." She frowned and leaned forward to peer at him. He seemed genuinely confused. "She wasn't at yours?"

"No." He clipped out the word like a bullet, and she had the distinct feeling he really disliked her. *That's good*, she told herself even though she wanted the opposite. So maybe she'd dreamt of him banging on her door in the dead of night—but for an entirely different reason.

She shook her head to clear it. Having fantasies about her sexy next-door neighbor wouldn't make sure Glenna's heat stayed on this winter.

"She was already in Jace's office when I got back there," she said. "I assumed she'd helped him with all the interviews."

Archer glared at her. He must practice for an hour every morning with how he'd perfected the narrow squint of his eyes and the extreme distaste pouring from every pore of his skin.

"Whatever," he finally said. "I just wanted you to know that I think you did a lousy thing today."

Her heart flopped like a fish on dry land. "I know I did, Archie. I'm sorry."

"Sometimes sorry—" He cut off as his phone sounded in tandem with hers. Her simple, factory-chosen chime didn't mesh with his custom *twill-a-will!* that echoed through the night sky after it finally finished.

He glanced at his phone; she at hers. Anything for a distraction.

This is Jace Lovell. Can you come for a second interview tomorrow at nine o'clock?

Her pulse catapulted around various points of her body, finally landing back in its rightful place in her chest. A smile pulled at the corners of her mouth, and she glanced up at Archer, who wore a grin so delightful she wondered what it felt like to be that happy.

"I have a second interview tomorrow," he said.

"Me too." She twisted her phone so he could see the message from Jace.

His smile vanished, replaced by a scowl and then a frown of confusion. "Mine's at nine too. That makes no sense."

"Maybe it's a group interview?" she guessed.

He wandered around the partition separating their front doors, his attention on his phone. He went inside without saying anything, almost like he'd forgotten Emery even stood there. With the final click of his door, she pushed hers closed too, her headache now pounding through her whole body.

She could only hope and pray he'd forgive her, just like

she'd been hoping and praying he'd finally wake up and *see* her standing right where she'd always been—next door.

———

Read THE CHRISTMAS COWBOY COMPETITION today! He's a cowboy down on his luck, she's his complete opposite next door, and they both need a job this Christmas…

Scan the QR code below to get it!

BOOKS IN THE HORSESHOE HOME RANCH ROMANCE SERIES:

The Redesigned Ranch (Book 1): Jace Lovell, still nursing a wounded heart after being jilted at the altar, has dedicated himself to becoming the best foreman at Horseshoe Home Ranch. When he decides to hire an interior designer to please the ranch owner's wife, he didn't expect to be faced with a familiar face from his past. **Can Belle's patience and faith help Jace find the path to forgiveness and lead them to discover their own slice of happily-ever-after?**

Snowed in with the Cowboy (Book 2): Sterling Maughan, once a renowned snowboarder, is in self-imposed exile at his family cabin after a tragic accident stole his career. Lost and without purpose, solitude is his only companion until an unexpected visitor disrupts his isolation. **Can Norah trust Sterling enough to let him into her life and give their unexpected and forbidden love a chance?**

The Preacher's Daughter (Book 3): Landon Edmunds, a cowboy born and bred, has had his rodeo dreams realized and then dashed by a career-ending injury. Back in his hometown working at Horseshoe Home Ranch, he yearns for a new beginning with a ranch of his own. His sights are set on buying a horse ranch to train rodeo horses, but his plans take a detour when his high school best friend, Megan Palmer, steps back into his life. **Will they choose to follow their hearts, or will they let true love slip through their fingers again?**

Be sure to check out the spinoff series, the Brush Creek Cowboys romances after you read THE PREACHER'S DAUGHTER. Start with BRUSH CREEK COWBOY.

The Cowboy and the Nanny (Book 4): Twelve years ago, Owen Carr traded his roots and his sweetheart in Gold Valley for the bright lights of Nashville, where he found fame as a country music star. But when a tragic accident leaves him single-handedly raising his eight-year-old niece, Marie, he's forced to return home. Overwhelmed and out of his depth, Owen finds a lifeline in a most unexpected place. **As they mend bridges and explore the sparks that still sizzle between them, will they open their hearts to a second chance at love?**

Right Cowboy, Right Time (Book 5): Caleb Chamberlain, a fun-loving cowboy at Horseshoe Home Ranch, has spent the last five years wrestling with the ghosts of his past—a devastating breakup, alcoholism, and a near-fatal accident. Now, he's finally found solace in laughter and the rhythmic simplicity of ranch life. But a chance encounter with a familiar face threatens to upheave his newfound peace. **Can they navigate the shadows of the past to find their happily-ever-after?**

Second Chance Family (Book 6): Ty Barker has been living a carefree existence for the last thirty years. As friends around him found love and started families, Ty filled his time by giving horseback riding lessons and serving on a community service committee. But beneath the jovial surface, he's starting to feel the sting of loneliness. **He knows he wants River Lee in his life—but the question is, can he navigate the delicate steps needed to make her stay with him?**

The Christmas Cowboy Competition (Book 7): Archer Bailey has already had to yield one job to Emersyn "Emery" Enders. So when the opportunity of a cowhand job at Horseshoe Home Ranch presents itself, he keeps it to himself. Emery, whose temporary job is ending but whose responsibilities towards her physically disabled sister aren't, is left in the dark.

As the festive season unfolds, **will Emery and Archer navigate the complexities of the ranch, their close living arrangements, and their personal challenges to discover the love building between them? Or will their rivalry rob them of the greatest Christmas gift of all—true love?**

USA Today Bestselling Author

LIZ ISAACSON

Love at First Cowboy

Love at First Cowboy (Book 8): Elliott Hawthorne, a career cowboy, has just witnessed his best friend and cabinmate forsake bachelorhood for matrimony. He'd be joyous if he weren't so green with envy. When a call about a family accident demands his presence, Elliott finds himself rushing from the ranch to his parents' house to see what's going on with his daddy, where he encounters the most stunning woman he's ever laid eyes on. **But as they encounter the complex dynamics of family responsibilities and personal desires, can their love-at-first-sight grow strong enough withstand the test of time?**

BOOKS IN THE BRUSH CREEK COWBOY ROMANCE SERIES:

Brush Creek Cowboy (Book 1): Former rodeo champion and cowboy Walker Thompson trains horses at Brush Creek Horse Ranch, where he lives a simple life in his cabin with his ten-year-old son. A widower of six years, he's worked with Tess Wagner, a widow who came to Brush Creek to escape the turmoil of her life to give her seven-year-old son a slower pace of life. But Tess's breast cancer is back…

Walker will have to decide if he'd rather spend even a short time with Tess than not have her in his life at all. Tess wants to feel God's love and power, but can she discover and accept God's will in order to find her happy ending?

The Cowboy's Challenge (Book 2): Cowboy and professional roper Justin Jackman has found solitude at Brush Creek Horse Ranch, preferring his time with the animals he trains over dating. With two failed engagements in his past, he's not really interested in getting his heart stomped on again. But when flirty and fun Renee  Martin picks him up at a church ice cream bar--on a bet, no less--he finds himself more than just a little interested. His Gen-X attitudes are attractive to her; her Millennial behaviors drive him nuts. Can Justin look past their differences and take a chance on another engagement?

A Cowboy Proposal (Book 3): Ted Caldwell has been a retired bronc rider for years, and he thought he was perfectly happy training horses to buck at Brush Creek Ranch. He was wrong. When he meets April Nox, who comes to the ranch to hide her pregnancy from all her friends back in Jackson Hole, Ted realizes he has a huge family-shaped hole in his life. April is embarrassed, heartbroken, and trying to find her extinguished faith. She's never ridden a horse and wants nothing to do with a cowboy ever again. Can Ted and April create a family of happiness and love from a tragedy?

A New Family for the Cowboy (Book 4): Blake Gibbons oversees all the agriculture at Brush Creek Horse Ranch, sometimes moonlighting as a general contractor. When he meets Erin Shields, new in town, at her aunt's bakery, he's instantly smitten. Erin moved to Brush Creek after a divorce that left her penniless, homeless, and a

single mother of three children under age eight. She's nowhere near ready to start dating again, but the longer Blake hangs around the bakery, the more she starts to like him. Can Blake and Erin find a way to blend their lifestyles and become a family?

The Cowboy and the Champion (Book 5): Emmett Graves has always had a positive outlook on life. He adores training horses to become barrel racing champions during the day and cuddling with his cat at night. Fresh off her professional rodeo retirement, Molly Brady comes to Brush Creek Horse Ranch as Emmett's protege. He's not thrilled, and she's allergic to cats. Oh, and she'd like to stay cowboy-free, thank you very much. But Emmett's about as cowboy as they come…. Can Emmett and Molly work together without falling in love?

Schooled by the Cowboy (Book 6): Grant Ford spends his days training cattle—when he's not camped out at the elementary school hoping to catch a glimpse of his ex-girlfriend. When principal Shannon Sharpe confronts him and asks him to stay away from the school, the spark between them is instant and hot. Shannon's  expecting a transfer very soon, but she also needs a summer outdoor coordinator—and Grant fits the bill. Just because he's handsome and everything Shannon's ever wanted in a cowboy husband means nothing. Will Grant and Shannon be able to survive the summer or will the Utah heat be too much for them to handle?

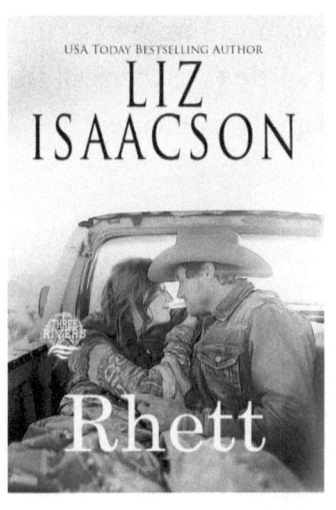

Rhett (Book 1): To save her business, she'll have to risk her heart. She needs a husband to be credible as a matchmaker. He wants to help a neighbor. **Will their fake marriage take them out of the friend zone?**

Tripp (Book 2): She needs a husband to keep her son. He's wanted to take their relationship to the next level, but she's always pushing him away. Will their trivial tie take them all the way to happily-ever-after?

Liam (Book 3): She's desperate to save her ranch. He wants to help her any way he can. Will their invented I-Do open doors that have previously been closed and lead to a happily-ever-after for both of them?

Jeremiah (Book 4): He wants to prove to his brothers that he's not broken. She just wants him. Will a fake marriage heal him or push her further away?

Wyatt (Book 5): To get her inheritance, she needs a husband. He's wanted to fly with her for ages. Can their pretend pledge turn into something real?

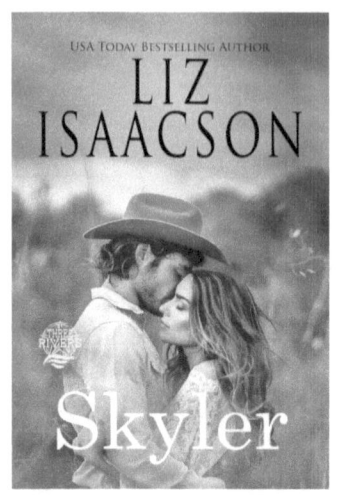

Skyler (Book 6): She needs a new last name to stay in school. He's willing to help a fellow student. Can this wanna-be wife show the playboy that some things should be taken seriously?

Micah (Book 7): They were just actors auditioning for a play. The marriage was just for the audition – until a clerical error results in a legal marriage. Can these two ex-lovers negotiate this new ground between them and achieve new roles in each other's lives?

Gideon (Book 8): It's 1971, and Gideon Walker is on the cutting edge of all the technology coming out of Texas. He has big dreams and wants to make something of himself. Then he meets Penny Aarons, and everything changes. He only has eyes for her, but she's got plans and dreams of her own...

Read this origin romance for Momma and Daddy from the Seven Sons series today!

Graham (Book 1): A cowboy returning to his hometown—and the best friend he left a dozen years before. This Christmas, can Graham and Laney build a family and find their happily-ever-after?

Eli (Book 2): A man who's traded his power suits for cowboy boots has feelings for his nanny...can Eli and Meg find love this Christmas?

Andrew (Book 3): A public relations director who moonlights as a cowboy, the woman who dislikes him and his energy company, and the job that could bring Andrew and Becca together...

Beau (Book 4): A cowboy lawyer turned bodyguard...including the celebrity country singer looking for a quick and quiet resolution to her problems. Can opposites Beau and Lily really attract this Christmas?

Todd (Book 5): A billionaire bull rider and the pretty country music singer he's boarding with...Can Todd and VI make the best of a difficult situation and maybe even find love this Christmas?

Liam (Book 6): A holiday bachelor auction brings a cowboy billionaire doctor and a country music star together. Will Rose and Liam be able to navigate their opposites to find a future together?

Finn (Book 7): Her sons want her to be happy, but she's too old to be set up on a blind date...isn't she? Can Amanda and Finn make their blind date into lasting love?

Zach (Book 8): Celia is finally ready to date again—but not the man whose family has a century-old feud with hers... Can Celia and Zach really make their *Romeo and Juliet* love story end in love and not tragedy?

ABOUT LIZ

Liz Isaacson writes inspirational romance, usually set in Texas, or Wyoming, or anywhere else horses and cowboys exist. She lives in Utah, where she writes full-time, takes her two dogs to the park everyday, and eats a lot of veggies while writing. Find her on her website at feelgoodfiction-books.com